Daniel W. Hood enjoys writing, photography, and cooking. He is a Tai Chi and Qigong practitioner and has studied Chinese martial arts for more than twenty years. Dan spent four years in the U.S. Air Force, and upon his discharge, he worked 39 years as a civil service employee, a television reporter, a photographer, and a disc jockey. A former amateur bodybuilder, Dan competed in a number of local contests and placed first in the Mr. Bay State and Mr. Massachusetts tall class competitions. He also placed 4th in the over-40 Mr. America contest.

Football Sequence Editing
Ryan Blissett, DMD, MMed SC
Harvard School of Dental Medicine
Michigan State University Alumni

Daniel W. Hood

Dancing with a Stranger

AUSTIN MACAULEY PUBLISHERS™
LONDON * CAMBRIDGE * NEW YORK * SHARJAH

Ordering Information
Quantity sales: Special discounts are available on quantity purchases by corporations, associations, and others. For details, contact the publisher at the address below.

Publisher's Cataloging-in-Publication data
Hood, Daniel W.
Dancing with a Stranger

ISBN 9798891553521 (Paperback)
ISBN 9798891553538 (ePub e-book)

Library of Congress Control Number: 2024905210

www.austinmacauley.com/us

First Published 2024
Austin Macauley Publishers LLC
40 Wall Street, 33rd Floor, Suite 3302
New York, NY 10005
USA

mail-usa@austinmacauley.com
+1 (646) 5125767

My sincere gratitude to Attorney Noel Richardson for his continuous support while I struggled to finish writing this book.

Chapter 1

Radio announcer's voice: *Good morning, New England. Well, it looks like we're in for another sizzler over this long holiday weekend. Temperatures all across the region are expected to climb from the low to mid-90s.*

It was the kind of weather that convinced Jane Furie to keep her hair pinned up on her head, something she usually did on hot, humid summer days.

Janey, a nickname given to her by a childhood friend, was a rather petite woman; five-foot-three inches tall with soft brown eyes that complemented her small nose and plump lips. The humidity in the air added a dewy, smooth texture to her skin.

There were several hobbies that she dreamed of doing while raising her son and helping her husband manage a growing insurance business in downtown Natick, Mass.

It wasn't very often that she had extra time on her hands, but when she did, she'd exercise or play Bingo at her local church.

The handsome mixed-race couple, and their 17-year-old son, David, looked forward to the weekend when they'd sit on the back porch and talk about their favorite hobby; football.

It wasn't just luck that David and Chris Wellman ended up living in houses a short distance away from each other. They had been friends ever since the fifth grade. A half-mile walk to Coolidge Field gave them a chance to play on the same Pop Warner football team.

The location was perfect, especially when the weather turned colder. And it served their parents well when they wanted to go walking, bike riding or shopping together.

***

Chapter 2

David's father played football at Colby College in Waterville, Maine. He was close to becoming an All-American tight end but a knee injury put an end to that dream.

While at Colby he was a wide back, muscled athlete, lean, and defined all the way down to his slender hips and waist.

Three years after graduating, he ballooned up to 270 pounds, chain-smoked and had a habit of overeating.

After huffing and puffing his way up a flight of stairs, he'd often mutter to himself, "I've just got to get back into the gym," which he never did.

Instead, after spending many long hours at his office, he'd come home, eat supper and fall asleep on the couch, mouth wide open, snoring loudly.

When weekends rolled around, he found time to pass his football knowledge on to his son.

He was surprised at how quickly he learned.

Except for football, all other daily happenings for David seemed insignificant.

Just like his father, football was always on his mind.

It was a different story for Jane. She could sit through a Sunday afternoon game, especially when the New England Patriots were playing. But she agreed with legendary humorist, Erma Bombeck, who once said:

Anybody who watches three games of football in a row should be declared brain dead.

Neither David nor his father thought it was unusual to watch that many games.

Using the remote, they'd constantly switch from one channel to another. After all, football was considered a 'manly man's sport' where players on opposing teams constantly reached explosive stages of testosterone rivalry.

When one game ended, and another began, she'd excuse herself and make a quick exit from her husband's beloved man cave.

She left it up to his beer drinking, cigar smoking friends to clean up the place afterwards.

As luck would have it, right in the middle of downtown Natick, sat Wellman's, the popular family-owned pharmacy and restaurant. It served as a meeting place for those who enjoyed munching on a mouth-watering plate of French fries, Buffalo chicken wings, or classic cheese burgers with sesame seeds on top.

At supper time, customers usually showed up for a plate of delicious baby-back ribs, mashed potatoes with gravy and a quick dose of neighborly news.

The pharmacy had somewhat of an old-fashioned look. Of the six secluded oak wood booths, three of them faced the ice cream counter. During lunch hour, they were usually occupied by beefy football players and their bubblegum-chewing girlfriends.

Despite the booth's overall thickness, secrets did not remain secrets very long.

There was a popular saying among students: *If you want to know what's going on in town, check out Wellman's.*

The never ending humming from the air conditioner near the entrance was often drowned out by two Bose loudspeakers.

Oldies music about teenage love and hot-and-heavy, backseat romance warmed the cool morning air.

Besides football, hanging out there was the only other constant in David's life.

It didn't take him long to learn that very few things in life are constant.

When he wasn't in school, or playing football, David's best friend, Chris, spent time behind the ice cream counter helping his father.

Other than David's dark, rugged features and curly hair, most people thought they were brothers.

On the football field, they were a perfect match. Many of Chris's pinpoint passes landed in David's hands, most of which he turned into touchdowns.

Wellman's, Saturday Afternoon, 3:00 PM

"Hey Chris, what's up?" David called out, scooping a couple of red cherries out of a glass bowl and popping them into his mouth.

"After you finish working, whaddya say we go over to Coolidge Field and practice."

"Sounds good to me," Chris replied, placing a tub of vanilla ice cream into the freezer. "I'll be through in a couple of minutes."

"Did anything exciting happen here today?"

"Not much, unless you want to call a brief appearance by Alesha Cross exciting."

"You gotta be kidding. What was she doing in this part of town?"

"Filling a prescription for her father, and picking up a half pint of chocolate ice cream," he answered, grabbing a towel and wiping some remnants off of his fingers.

"Was she by herself?"

"No—not exactly. Her father sat outside in his car and honked a couple of times. After she paid for the ice cream, she split without saying a word to anyone."

"If she likes chocolate ice cream as much as I do, I bet she'll be back for more. Then I'll get a chance to check her out."

Chris untied his apron and dropped it into a receptacle beneath the counter. "I wouldn't count on it because, most likely, he'll be with her."

"He must have a hell of a good reason for keeping close tabs on her."

"Maybe it's because he's a very prominent Appeals Court judge who strongly believes in social and municipal reform."

"That's possible. It could also have a lot to do with his reputation, like he doesn't want her hanging around creeps like us."

"Could be," replied Chris, reaching beneath the counter.

He pulled out a football and tossed it at David, who caught it with one hand.

"We've got an important game coming up in a couple of days," he said, "so let's get out of here."

Chapter 3

David was awakened early the next morning by the smell of freshly brewed coffee, scrambled eggs, and bacon wafting up from the kitchen.

He took several deep breaths of fresh air blowing in from his bedroom window before taking a shower. Then he slipped into a pair of faded jeans and a jersey with the New England Patriot's logo on the front.

A narrow hall and a flight of stairs led to a kitchen on one side, a bedroom, a reception hall, and a dining room on the other.

He wasn't surprised to see his father sitting at the kitchen table scoffing down a side of pancakes drowned in maple syrup.

After exchanging greetings, David dished up some eggs, and glanced at his father, who was busy digesting the news on the front page of the Boston Voice.

"Where's Mom?" he asked.

"She went to the gym early, so she can get home in time to watch the Pats."

"What time is the game?"

"One o'clock. But before it starts, I have a little job for you," he said, lighting a cigarette and taking a long drag.

"Sure, what is it?"

"I promised a couple of my clients that I'd drop off their insurance policies today."

"Got a little busy at the office last week, huh?"

"Yeah—lots of renewals."

"And you want me to drive?"

"I think it'd take your mind off of your upcoming game against Brockton Tech," he replied, crushing out his old cigarette and lighting another.

"It's going to be a tough game," said David, watching his father run his hand through his hair in a way that he had grown to recognize as a nervous habit.

"I think we'll be OK," he replied.

"I hope so," he said, sliding his car keys across the table. "We'll leave as soon as you finish your breakfast."

"No problem."

Chapter 4

David's conversations with his father about football were usually sprinkled with witty, original, finished phrases of general interest. He was listening to everything his father said until he turned off the road onto a long secluded driveway.

The scent of pine and dahlias was thick in the morning air.

A double gated entrance allowed access to plenty of parking and turning space.

Gracefully situated on a serene hilltop sat a huge mansion connected on the north side with the city, and open on the south to a beautiful and boundless horizon.

The exquisitely terraced grounds included stone walls, an orchard, and fountains, along with a swimming pool and a hot tub.

A pool house cabana overlooked two tennis courts.

"Wow!" said David, his eyes widening at the sight of the luxurious mansion. "This place must be worth at least two million."

"Two and a half to be exact," said his father, hopping out of the car. "I'll be back in fifteen to twenty minutes."

"OK," he answered, settling back in his chair.

Sitting alone in a strange place made David restless.

He stared at the shrubbery and flowers that dotted both sides of the driveway.

All had been meticulously pruned and dripped moisture from an earlier watering.

He reached into the backseat and grabbed his football.

I don't think anyone will mind if I just stand outside and toss my football around.

That's what he thought until a huge bull mastiff came skidding around the corner of the cabana.

Muscles rippling under its close cropped hair, bared fangs, and growling, it headed straight for him.

"Holy shit," he said, quickly jumping back into the car and rolling up the windows.

The bull mastiff wasn't far behind. He jumped at the door and began scratching on the window.

From behind his car, he heard someone shout, "GET DOWN, BRUTUS, GET DOWN!"

He turned his head and looked out the back window. A short distance away, he spotted a girl dressed in a white tennis outfit.

She had a very concerned look on her face.

She ran up to his car, grabbed Brutus's collar, and tried to pull him away from the door. But she was no match for the 120 pound dog.

"Get back, damn it. Get back!" she screamed.

Brutus was moving with so much speed, he simply brushed her aside like a bag full of feathers.

She lost her balance and fell.

David had seen enough. He rolled down his window, grabbed his football and poked Brutus in the nose.

"BEAT IT!" he yelled.

Much to his surprise, Brutus yelped, backed away from the car, and beat a fast track down the driveway and out of sight.

David pushed open his door and jumped out. "Are you all right?" he asked.

"I'm OK. He didn't hurt me," she answered.

His fingers closed firmly around her arm, and he helped her up.

"Are you sure you're alright?"

"He was only doing what he was trained to do."

"Attack people?"

"It's my fault. Nobody ever visits us on Sunday. I thought it'd be OK to let him out of his kennel so we could go for a walk."

"That was sort of a weird way to get acquainted. Mind if I ask you your name?"

"Not at all," she answered, brushing her hair back from her face. "Alesha Cross."

Standing close to her, revealed her warm beauty, her chiseled features, long black hair and sparkling brown eyes.

He felt his heart skip a beat, and he stared at her for a couple of seconds.

In addition to having a rare combination of earthy sensuality and icy aloofness, she was also exotically beautiful.

Chris is not going to believe this.

"Now that I've told you my name, what's yours?" she asked.

It was like walking from reality into a dream and back again and he finally answered.

"Ah—mine's David—David Furie."

"Nice meeting you, David Furie," she said in a sweet voice, showing her white teeth and blinking her eyes pleasantly.

He reached out to shake her hand and realized that his football was still tucked beneath his arm. "I hope I didn't hurt your dog."

"Buster's bark is worse than—"

"His bite," he chimed in.

They laughed simultaneously.

"So, what brings you here on such a beautiful Sunday morning?" she asked, lifting a hand to shade her eyes from the sun.

"My father had to drop off an insurance policy."

"It's really hot out here. And since I believe that hot weather fries people's brains, let's go sit by the pool," she suggested. "It's much cooler there."

"Show me the way," he replied, his assessing gaze taking in the beauty of the surrounding area. "I've never seen such a beautiful place as this."

Her smile faded and her expression turned gloomy.

"It's OK," she said, casually tipping her head and looking up at him.

The ground beneath the parasol was checkered with sunlight and shade.

A pitcher of ice cold lemonade sat in the center of the table.

She filled two glasses and handed one to him.

"Thanks," he said, taking a sip. "A couple of minutes ago, you sounded like you didn't like living here."

"I do. But there's more to life than all of this luxury," she replied.

"Like what?"

"Like love."

Her answer surprised him and he watched her face with a puzzled expression.

"I don't quite understand."

"I'm sorry. I should have kept my big mouth shut."

"No—it's OK. Would you like to talk about what's bugging you?"

He was shocked at the sheer venom of her reply.

"I hate my father."

At first, he didn't know how to respond. Then an interesting thought entered his mind.

If she tells me more about her personal life, maybe I'll get to know her better, and we'll see each other again.

"Those are very strong words."

"I know. But you'd probably hate yours too if he yelled at you all the time. And threatened to send you away if he caught you hanging out with what he calls *lowlifes*."

"Who do you think he's talking about?"

"People who he considers socially inferior or who don't live up to his expectations."

He frowned. "I can understand his concern. But I don't think he realizes that they're not everywhere that you go."

"He thinks they are."

"Then he's living in a world that's a hell of a lot different than ours."

She struggled to control her emotions as the next few words came out.

"My mother is almost as bad as he is. It's one of the many oddities about her that I've learned to accept over the years."

"Isn't she capable of speaking for herself?"

"It'd be great if she did. But whenever his blood pressure goes up and he starts yelling and swearing at us, all she does is retreat to another part of the house."

"It must be tough living under the same roof with him."

"It is. I usually go to bed around two in the morning. Bad thoughts about him come and go and I toss about till dawn."

She picked up her glass and took another sip, her eyes searching his over the rim.

"Some days are like spending twenty-four hours in hell."

"I don't think it's unusual for three people living in the same house to not get along sometimes, but not constantly."

"If you lived here, I doubt if you'd feel that way."

He shrugged his shoulders. "Maybe I would, I don't know."

"My mother has such a mild temper that, even if he speaks harshly to her, she endures it and never retaliates. It's different with me. His temper tantrums caused me to have nightmares."

"How bad were they?"

She swallowed hard, images from her nightmares returning.

"There was one in particular that kept occurring over and over again. I dreamed that these strange creatures in black robes were chasing me and I hid behind a tombstone. But they always find me. When I try to escape, the tombstone slowly begins to open and I start to fall into this dark hole. I know something's down there waiting for me, but there's nothing to grab onto. Before I fall in, I notice the name on the tombstone is mine."

Her words caused the hair on the back of his neck to prickle. "That'd probably scare the hell out of anybody."

"It scared me so much, I was afraid my heart would stop beating."

"Did you tell your mother about it?"

"When I did, she sent me to a clinic. After a couple of weeks, the doctor told her that I was suffering from amenorrhea, which he thought might be related to depression, or some other kind of mental problem. So he referred me to a psychiatrist for further evaluation."

"What did your father say after she told him that he might be the cause of some of your problems?"

She chewed the bottom of her lip as she considered the question.

"He said I was just acting out. Then he told me—ah, sorry, 'to get my head out of my ass' or he'd send me to a boarding school. Like, how mean can that be? I never understood why she married him."

"Maybe it's because women have needs and desires that men don't quite understand."

She knotted her eyebrows together. "I'm sorry, but I don't think that's the reason."

A long, soft ripple of wind flowed over the pool, and brought a puff of warm autumn air into their faces.

"Enough about them, for now," she said. "Tell me something about yourself."

He smiled. "There's not a heck of a lot to tell."

"Oh, come on," she said, filling up his glass again. "When I first saw you, you were tossing around a football. You're a pretty big guy so you're either a football player a wrestler or something like that."

"I'm a football player."

"What team do you play for?"

"Natick North Hawks," he said proudly.

"I don't know much about football. But I'd love to see you play."

Her words floored and excited him for more reasons than one.

"That'd be great. We've got a big game at Natick High this Saturday; starts at 1 o'clock. Think you can make it?"

"I think so. I'll hook up with my girlfriend so my father won't object."

Someone's voice interrupted their conversation. From a balcony overlooking the pool stood a rather attractive, well-dressed woman.

She shaded her eyes with the back of her hand.

"Alesha, Alesha! It's almost time to go!" she yelled.

Alesha peeked out from beneath the parasol. "Hold on," she shouted. "I'll be there in a minute!"

"Gotta go, huh?" he asked, taking in her warm features and shapely body.

"It's my mother. We're going to Boston to get our hair done."

"I really enjoyed our conversation."

"Me too," she replied.

"I hope it's not our last," he said with a mesmerizing smile.

She blushed, realizing he was returning her smile. "I'll look for you after the game."

"You know where Wellman's is? I'll be right there waiting outside."

"OK. Now I've really got to go," she said, kissing him on the cheek, his mind racing with what he had just learned about Alesha Cross.

Chapter 5

An estimated ten thousand people showed up for the game. When David and his team mates jogged onto the field, the noise was so terrific it nearly caused some of them to jump out of their skin. It sounded more like the din of war, instead of a football game.

In the fourth quarter, David's team was trailing Brockton Tech 28-14.

But the Hawks responded with a nine-play, 66-yard scoring drive capped off with a 25-yard touchdown pass from Chris to David.

Back came Brockton.

They marched just outside of the red zone after their quarterback completed two third-down passes for first downs. That bruising drive came to an end when a Natick linebacker sacked their quarterback.

But they rebounded quickly, forcing a three-and-out, putting them on Natick's 40.

With less than a minute remaining on the game clock, their coach called a time-out.

That gave David and Chris enough time to trot over to the sideline and discuss a defensive play that might put the ball back in their hands.

"OK guys, no need to panic," said their coach. "They're still a pretty good distance from our goal line. My guess is that they're going to run an option play so we've got to keep their quarterback from running out of the pocket. Our front line will blitz him and you guys will stick to their receivers just in case he throws the ball. We've got to keep them from getting within field goal range. Just make sure they don't get that touchdown; make sure we win. Got it?"

They nodded in agreement and trotted back onto the field.

"Listen up, guys," whispered Chris to his teammates. "Coach wants us to use a four-three blitz on their quarterback, and man-to-man coverage on receivers. Let's do this!"

"Hawks!" they shouted in unison, clapping their hands and lining up in front of the Brockton's offensive line.

On the very first play, the Brockton quarterback faded back—looked left, then right. From his blind side, a Natick linebacker avoided a block and broke through their line.

Realizing that he was very close to being sacked, he ran out of the pocket and tossed the football. It turned out to be a bad decision. His receiver juggled the football. David batted it in the air, and much to his surprise, it came down in his arms.

From the Natick side of the field, a sudden roar erupted as he jetted back up field with half of Brockton's players in hot pursuit.

He felt someone touch his shoulder, but he didn't dare look back.

Brockton's disgruntled receiver was right on his heels.

Chris cut back across the field and threw a bone-crushing block that knocked him off his feet. That allowed David to cross the goal line just as the scoreboard lit up: **TOUCHDOWN. NATICK, 27; BROCKTON, 28.**

With no time-outs left and only five seconds remaining on the game clock, Natick had to make a quick decision; settle for a tie and force the game into overtime or go for a two-point conversion.

Chris glanced over at his coach. He seemed to know the answer: a two-point conversion.

"They're pissed because we stole the ball so if you guys can hold your blocks a little longer, we'll win this game, OK?"

All the Natick players nodded their heads; their temples throbbed with excitement.

"We've worked on this play all week, so it should work. Jones Special on two," said Chris quietly, a confident look on his face.

The tension between both teams was thick, their heat filling the empty space between them.

He lined up over his center and studied Brockton's defense. "Hut one, hut two!" he yelled.

The football snapped back in his hands. He held it tightly, faded back and fired a rocket just as David cut across the middle.

The jarring sound of shoulder pads and bodies surrounded him.

The football was a little bit in front of David, but he stretched out and snagged it before it hit the ground.

The scoreboard glittered 0:00, with no time remaining.

NATICK, 29; BROCKTON, 28.

Natick had successfully stuffed the two-point conversion, giving them the win.

The final whistle was greeted with cheers of jubilation and sighs of relief.

Seconds later, David found himself buried beneath an avalanche of overjoyed teammates.

He squeezed his body out from beneath them, a large grin on his face. "Great job, guys! Great job!"

His coach ran over and slapped him on the back. "That was a hell of a catch!" he yelled over the din.

"Thanks coach. What a great way to start the season!" he replied.

"You can say that again! See you in the locker room."

Chapter 6

It was early evening, and the sidewalks were already packed with people headed to the small bistros, cafes and other outdoor eateries lining North Maine Street. An overflow crowd of football players jammed Wellman's, the traffic outside, thick and loud.

As soon as David and Chris arrived, the cheers and applause turned into a single, sustained roar.

"OK guys—don't forget, it was only our first game," smiled David. "So have a good time tonight, because it's back to work on Monday."

"Aren't you coming in?" asked Chris.

"I'll be in as soon as my date shows up."

"You've got a date?" he said, a surprised look on his face.

"Yes, and you're not going to believe me when I tell you who it is."

"I'm all ears."

He lowered his voice and answered, "Alesha Cross."

Chris shook his head disbelievingly. "I think you've taken too many hits in the head. Are you sure you're alright?"

"I'm fine."

"How the hell did you pull that one off?"

"I guess you could say that I was in the right place at the right time."

"What's she like? I mean, is she nice, or is she a snob like her father?"

Just as he was about to answer, a black Mercedes sedan rounded the corner and pulled over to the curb.

Alesha rolled down her window. A captivating smile crossed her lips.

She was dressed in an off-the-shoulder lilac-colored sundress, both of which immediately caught his attention.

Damn, she's beautiful, he thought to himself.

"Hi, David—sorry, we're a little late," she said. "The traffic on Main Street was horrible."

"Yeah—it's like that after every game."

"So, how would you guys like to get away from here and go for a ride?"
Chris didn't wait for an answer.

"We'd love to," he said, lowering his head and checking out the driver, a stunning girl with long dark lashes and brown curly hair.

She wiggled her fingers at him.

"Hi, I'm Jenny, Alesha's best friend. As soon as she climbs into the backseat with David, you can sit next to me. Then we'll grab a couple of pizzas and have our own little victory party at Cochituate State Park."

"Sounds good to me; let's go," said David, opening the back door for Alesha.

***

They found a table and bench at the far end of the park and munched on two large pizzas washed down with a six-pack of Coke.

An hour later, the sun appeared on the horizon and disappeared behind a mixture of long, narrow pink and blue clouds that hung above it.

David felt it was a good time to let Chris and Jenny get to know each other.

"Hey bro," he said. "I hope you and Jenny don't mind if we walk down to the pond."

"No prob," he replied, winking his eye. "The park closes in about a half an hour. So we'll meet you back here."

Alesha reached for David's hand and felt an instant warm rush when she found it.

"I'm so glad to see you again," she said.

"Me too," he replied in a quiet voice; kissing her on the cheek. "Before I started playing football, my dad and I used to come here all the time, and run around these hills."

"That explains why you're so fast on your feet."

He smiled down at her sweetly. "To be honest, most of the time, I'm running for my life."

A soft laugh escaped her throat. "Well congratulations, you played a great game."

"Thanks," he said, squeezing her hand affectionately.

They stopped beneath a large oak tree that leaned over the pond with outstretched branches, as if ready to catch a fish.

She let go of his hand and slipped off her sneakers.

"I love the feeling of sand beneath my feet and the water looks so inviting."

"Go ahead—dip your feet in."

"Are you sure it's OK?"

"Sure I'm sure, go ahead."

"I don't get a chance very often to do something like this."

"Well, now's your chance."

"OK, if you insist," she replied, stepping into the water.

Gentle waves licked at her ankles.

Suddenly, she screamed, grabbed his arm, and jumped back out.

"Something slimy brushed up against my ankle!"

He wrapped his arms around her in a tight hug to keep her from falling.

"It was probably a school of minnows feeding close to shore."

"Whatever it was scared the crap out of me."

Suddenly, they realized how close their bodies were pressed against each other.

He pulled her even closer, his lips warm against hers.

She returned his kiss, her mouth partially opened.

Her breath smelled sweet, almost as if she had just brushed her teeth with peppermint tooth paste.

She waited for him to release her, but his lips moved across her cheek and down her neck with soft, caressing kisses.

She turned her head away and whispered in his ear.

"David honey, we're going to be in big trouble if we keep this up."

He backed away from her.

"I'm sorry. I shouldn't have started—"

She pressed her index finger against his lips, interrupting him.

"No need to apologize. It's as much my fault as it is yours."

"We'd better go back so we don't miss our ride."

As they approached Jenny's car, they noticed a commotion going on at the front gate.

In the distance and getting closer, they heard the sound of police sirens and in minutes, two cruisers pulled into the driveway.

The air was filled with marijuana smoke and the scent of sweaty bodies.

Jenny and Chris sat quietly in her car a concerned look on their faces.

David and Alesha climbed in and he placed his arm protectively on the back of the seat behind her neck.

"What's up?" he asked.

"The people in that car in front of us just got busted for pot," Chris answered. "Now the police are searching everyone's car."

"Yeah, we smelled it as soon as we got closer to the exit."

"Hey, hey you there!" an officer shouted briskly, pointing at Jenny.

"Get out of line and pull your car over to the guard's shack!"

Everyone felt a little sense of nervousness. But Jenny did as she was told knowing that none of them had anything to hide.

She opened the glove compartment and took out her registration.

"That cop looks like he's having a bad day," David said.

"I was thinking the same thing," she said. "So let's be nice so we don't piss him off even more."

A dark form moved toward Jenny's car, shining a flashlight in her direction. The light reflected off more than one pair of eyes. It blinded them for a moment.

An officer approached the driver's side, and Jenny held up her hand, shielding her eyes from the glare.

He bent over, stuck a beefy hand inside the window and looked directly at her.

"License and registration," he said, an irritated edge to his voice.

She handed them to him.

"After you open the trunk, all of you get out and stand beside your car."

"No problem," she replied, pressing the trunk release button.

He walked around to the back of her car and his head disappeared behind the trunk lid.

It remained there for several minutes before he slammed down the lid and continued to search the interior of the car.

Shortly after, he returned Jenny's license and registration.

He waved his flashlight in an arc above their heads, first glancing at Chris, then David.

"I'm glad you're all clean because I wouldn't want to drag you two football stars and your girlfriends into the station."

Jenny smiled. "You recognize them, huh?"

"Of course, I recognize them. Their pictures are plastered on the front page of every newspaper in town. You guys played a great game."

His compliment brought smiles to their faces.

"Thank you, sir," David said.

The glow from his flashlight and the emergency lights from the police cars illuminated the next few feet of darkness.

Then, in the beam of his flashlight, her face partially hidden behind David's broad shoulders, stood Alesha.

The officer's tone was unassuming, but his gaze was intent, like he was trying to determine if he recognized her or not.

"You look familiar. What's your name?"

Hear twice before you speak once, she thought before answering.

He repeated his question.

"Just in case you didn't hear me the first time—what's your name?"

He moved closer to David and stared down at her.

She looked up. Fear clutched her heart.

"What are you, deaf, dumb or just plain stupid?" he asked.

David had to think fast. *Oh, oh—he's going to recognize her.*

"She didn't answer, sir, because she's deaf," he said, squeezing her hand to comfort her.

The officer nodded absently, giving her one last questioning look.

"Since you two lovebirds are standing so close to each other, I assume you're her boyfriend?"

"Yes, sir."

"Then you wouldn't mind telling me her name."

He answered in a voice that trembled a little.

"It's Dolley—Dolley Madison."

"You kids probably don't know it, but she has an identical twin."

"Really?" said Chris, looking genuinely surprised.

"Yeah, she lives a couple of miles down the road."

Jenny raised her arm, wiggled her fingers, like she was using sign language to converse with Alesha.

She nodded and returned her own gesture.

"She wants you to know," replied Jenny, "that she's often mistaken for that person."

Her answer followed a momentary pause, which seemed very long to them all.

"OK, you can go now. But before you do, let me give you a little piece of advice," the officer said. "When you're here, try to stay away, as far as you can, from drug dealers, beggars and bums—understand?"

"Yes, sir," Jenny answered respectfully. "We will."

They piled into her car; she turned on the ignition and headed back to downtown Natick.

"Ever seen that officer before?" David asked.

"I think he came to our house a couple of times to drive my father to the courthouse," Alesha recalled.

"Has he ever come in close contact with you?"

"No."

"Then I guess we're OK."

Chris turned around in his seat and looked at David.

"So where'd you get the idea to call her Dolley Madison?"

"It's the first thing that came into my mind. And that sign language trick was also pretty cool. Hopefully, it fooled him. On top of that, I don't want Alesha to get into any trouble."

"I get it."

Ten minutes later, they were back at Wellman's.

Alesha pressed a piece of paper into his hand.

"Here's my phone number and my email. Call or text me so we can make a plan to see each other again."

"Definitely," he said.

"This has been a beautiful evening. Too bad it has to end here," she said, kissing his lips softly.

He smiled at the remembrance of their first kiss. "I'll be in touch," he said.

Before he had a chance to climb out of the car, she enveloped him in a warm hug that smelled of expensive perfume.

"I'll miss you," she whispered in his ear.

"I'll miss you, too. Take care until I see you again."

Chapter 7

The following week, David was so busy with his studies and football practice he barely had time to think about anything else.

Four days had passed before he finally decided to call Alesha.

When he did, she didn't answer.

Maybe I called the wrong number, he thought to himself. So he tried again with the same results.

He texted her quickly, typing with his thumbs. He listened to an automated message and sighed in frustration.

I'm sorry but this mailbox is full. Older text messages must be deleted before new text messages can be received.

Several seconds of confusion followed. *Oh well, I guess the only way I can find out what's going on is to email her.*

Another three days dragged by; still no answer.

He thought about driving by her house to see if he could catch a glimpse of her. But he changed his mind, knowing that his unexpected visit could get her in trouble.

***

Natick North won its second game on a day when the weather was raw, rainy and cool.

Although his team won by a fairly large margin, it was not one of his best efforts.

He caught one of Chris's pinpoint passes; was hit hard and fumbled.

Fortunately, it was recovered by one of his teammates.

Two plays later, he ran a similar pattern. The ball was within reach but it bounced off his fingertips and skidded out of bounds.

Come on man, he murmured to himself, *you're thinking too much about Alesha.*

Later at Wellman's, over a cheeseburger and a mouthful of fries, he and Chris talked about two things; the game and the girls.

"My timing was a little bit off today," he said. "I should've caught that pass. And that stupid fumble—"

Chris cut him off in mid-sentence.

"C'mon man, you're being too hard on yourself. The weather certainly didn't help."

"My father will never accept that kind of excuse."

Chris shrugged his shoulders and smiled.

"Well, perhaps you should come and live with me until the football season is over. Maybe then he'll get over it."

He intended that as a joke, but David merely shook his head; his face gloomy, his lips compressed.

Chris pointed at the door.

"You'll feel better after I tell you that Alesha and Jenny are waiting outside?"

Surprise trickled through David and his face lit up.

"Are you serious or is this another one of your freaking jokes?"

"If you don't believe me, go take a look for yourself. Alesha didn't want to come in, so Jenny and I will wait here until you guys make up for lost time."

"How long have you known this?"

"It doesn't matter. Just get your lazy ass up and go see her while you have a chance."

David bounced out of his seat and thanked Jenny with a big smile.

The minute Alesha saw him, a warm feeling rushed up her neck and broke over her cheeks.

A similar wave of emotion gripped his entire body after he climbed into the car and sat down beside her. His eyes were twinkling, but he maintained a sober expression.

She reached out to hug him, but he backed away.

"Apparently you're not glad to see me," she said, folding her hands in her lap.

"Should I be?"

"I get it. You're angry because I didn't answer my phone when you called."

"What'd you expect?"

"Would you mind if I tell you why I didn't—"

He cut her short. "I think I already know. It's all about your relationship with your father."

"You got half of that right."

"What about the other half?"

"The other half has to do with you."

"What do you mean?"

"Every boyfriend that I've ever had, were hand-picked by my father. And they were all creeps. Then you came along, and everything changed. You're the first guy that I've felt close to. And if my father ever found out that I was dating what he calls 'a lowlife' he'd go ballistic."

He let out an exasperated sigh. "He doesn't even know me."

"No, but it wouldn't take him long to find out everything about you. And that's when all hell would break loose. He'd follow through with his threats to send me away. Then it'd be a long time before we'd see each other again."

"It sounds like he has his own mean, irascible way of judging people."

"Not just people, but also where they live. You should hear the derogatory things he says about minorities. It's sickening."

Her father's a racist, he thought. Then he pushed the thought from his mind.

"So, where do we go from here?"

"That's exactly what I was thinking when I didn't answer my phone or your email."

"Between the two of us, we should be able to work out something."

"There's one thing for sure. I'm not going to let anyone, including my father, come between us."

He wrapped his arms around her tightly and kissed her deeply.

She gently broke the embrace and smiled at him in an inviting way.

"When you kiss me like that, you make my whole body tremble."

"Mine too."

"That kiss is going to have to last us for a while because tomorrow, my mother and I are going to New York to do a little shopping."

He cupped her cheeks in his hands.

"Promise that you'll stay in touch when you get back."

"I promise. Jenny's going to drive me home so I can do some packing. I'll miss you terribly."

"Take care," he said, drawing her into his arms and planting a soft kiss on her cheek.

Chapter 8

David arrived home a half hour later, his mind filled with happy thoughts about his growing relationship with Alesha.

Before he could unlock the door, it swung open.

His mother, her face a straight line of pain, opened her arms and embraced him.

"Thank goodness, you're home. I was just going to call you."

"What's wrong, Mom—what's wrong?"

"Your father suffered a heart attack," she answered, her voice trembling.

His mouth suddenly turned dry and he asked a complicated question. "How bad is it?"

"All I know is that right after your game, he wanted to stop downtown and treat his buddies to lunch," she answered, looking increasingly worried.

"That sounds just like him," he said, helping her on with her coat.

***

Upon arriving at the hospital, they were greeted by a nurse who accompanied them down a long drab corridor to the Cardiac Care Unit.

"Please have a seat. The doctor will be with you shortly," she said, her voice gentle and kind.

David closed his eyes tightly and swallowed around the lump in his throat. His mind full of negative thoughts:

How well is she functioning during this emergency? If my father dies, who'll run the insurance business? He'll never see me play college football.

They glanced up expectantly as the doctor strode toward Jane and gave her the bad news.

"Mrs. Furie, I'm Dr. Corrado. I just finished evaluating your husband's condition and as long as I've worked here, it has always been difficult to deliver bad news."

She let out a little gasp and clutched David's hand.

"When your husband was admitted, he already had rapidly deteriorating heart valves," he said, his voice quiet, and respectful, "My staff and I had to judge by his condition, how to administer treatment. We concluded that because of the amount of heart muscle that was permanently damaged, there wasn't much we could do, except make him comfortable."

"Can we see him?" she asked, hope still in her eyes.

"Yes, but please, don't do or say anything that will excite him."

The nurse took them across the hall to a private room and opened the door.

Maybe it was his father's looming death, or the energy from his mother's trembling touch that sent a message to David: *try to stay calm*. Tears were in his eyes, but he tried to look brave.

Fearful anticipation gripped Jane. She braced herself for what she was about to hear, the high-pitched sound of an electrocardiograph used to monitor her husband's heartbeat.

A priest stood nearby, stoic, bolt-straight and reading silently from the Bible.

This can't be happening, David thought, as his mother, her eyes red and puffy, looked up at him.

"Oh David, oh David," she cried.

He placed his hand on her shoulder and stared at his father's sallow face. *What do I say, what can I do?*

"David, David," he heard his father whisper. "That was a good game that you played today. Sorry that I got sick."

"You don't have to apologize, Dad."

His father's voice was weak, as if he were far away. David bent over, his ear close enough to hear.

"I guess the excitement was too much for me."

"When you get better, you and Mom will be at my next game. And I'll score a special touchdown for you guys."

Dr. Corrado entered the room, looked at a progress chart and mumbled a few words to the nurse.

David watched them closely, looking for some sign of hope in their faces, but he saw none.

"Dad, you don't have to worry about a thing while you're here. Mom's in good hands," he said reassuringly.

His father's voice trailed off to a sigh. "I know."

Jane lowered her head softly across his chest and began to sob loudly.

"Mom, Mom, I think we should let him rest now."

Suddenly, he realized that the electrocardiograph had stopped pulsating. Now there was nothing more than a straight, illuminated, green line that appeared across the glass enclosure in front.

The nurse looked at her watch, made a couple of notes on the medical chart and turned to Jane.

"I'm so sorry, I'm afraid he's gone."

David gripped his father's lifeless hand.

"He couldn't be gone. He was just talking to me."

"I know, but there wasn't much more that we could do for him," she replied.

Tears welled up in his eyes. He reached over and pressed his hands on his father's cheeks.

"Dad, Dad, don't be dead. Please don't be dead."

The priest placed a consoling hand on David's shoulder.

"There's a chapel down the hall if you'd like to go there and pray."

"Thank you, sir. But I'll stay with my mother until she's ready to leave."

Chapter 9
Three Weeks Later

Jane Furie lapsed into deep stages of depression during the long Thanksgiving weekend. She even stopped going to charity Bingo games at her church. And she didn't smile as much as she used to. Instead, she'd sit in her husband's favorite chair, handkerchief knotted around her fingers, tears in her eyes and watch television until she finally fell asleep.

Fortunately, the Wellmans helped straighten out legal and financial matters at the insurance office. That was a load off her back and gave her more time to recover from the shock of her husband's sudden death.

Upon her return from New York, Alesha called David several times to express her deepest sympathies on the death of his father.

He desperately wanted to see her, but preparations for his college entrance exams kept him up late at night. He was also worried about his mother, who had lost a significant amount of weight.

Eventually, boredom set in. Most of the friends that his parents once knew disappeared, leaving them with just a few unforgettable memories.

Chapter 10

The next few weeks rolled by slowly. During that time, something happened that was perhaps inevitable. Tired of sitting at home grieving, Jane decided to attend a charity fundraising event at her church. And there, she met a pretty suave, slightly sophisticated man.

His name was Bill Parham.

He was the kind of guy who considered himself irresistible to the ladies.

His stylish haircut, his swagger, his smooth talk, and the backseat of his ten-year-old Buick Riviera served him well.

When he introduced himself to Jane, there was something about the way he looked at her, the emotion that stirred within her when they shook hands.

The scent of his shaving lotion tickled her senses, his nearness made her warm body feel even warmer.

What impressed her even more was his donation of ten thousand dollars to the church's charity fundraising drive.

He didn't waste any time asking her out for dinner. But she felt that things were moving too fast, even though her heart fluttered at his words. And she grew excited about him wanting to pursue a friendly relationship.

***

David soon noticed that an expression of profound sorrow suddenly began to disappear from his mother's face, and curiosity overcame him.

"You don't seem to be quite as sad as you were a couple of months ago," he said.

She smiled slightly. "I miss your father terribly, but sitting inside week after week isn't going to bring him back. So I decided to resume my church activities."

"Yeah, I know what you mean. I think about him whenever I touch a football."

A brief silence followed before she spoke again. "Yes, I know." Then she quickly changed the subject. "Oh, I almost forgot. Mrs. Wellman is picking me up in a couple of minutes so we can help out at a charity event at the church, so I might be a little late getting home."

"No problem. See you later."

Now that the house was quiet, David decided to tackle his college entrance exams.

An hour later, his head flopped over on his chest and he fell asleep in front of his computer.

Around midnight, he was awakened by the sound of a car door slamming shut.

He glanced at his watch and was surprised to see how late it was.

He peeked out his window and caught sight of his mother in the light of the passenger's door as it opened.

A well-dressed man in his prime with mixed gray hair emerged from the driver's side.

They stood outside talking for several minutes, their conversation a mixture of interest and handshakes, before he kissed her on the cheek, climbed back in his car and drove off.

Curiosity got the best of him.

"Hi Mom," he called out, as the front door slammed shut behind her. "Have a good time?"

"Yes, I did," she answered. "You're up awful late."

"Yeah—I thought I'd catch up on my exams."

Passing a mirror, she glanced into it and pushed her hair back from her face. "Honey, do you think I'm pretty?"

"You're the prettiest woman in this whole town. Why'd you ask?"

"Because a couple of weeks ago, I met a very nice man, and he asked me out."

"You're talking about the guy who drove you home, right?"

"Yes."

Now that he was the head of the family, he felt that the welfare of his mother would always be of paramount importance.

"What does he do for a living?"

"He works for a charity organization. He said that a lot of famous movie actors and models are donors."

Were his comments genuine or simply a way to get her to like him?

"Do you plan to see him again?"

She shrugged her shoulders.

"I guess so. But he's not someone that I plan to—well, you know—get involved with."

"I don't have to know that," he replied, feeling a bit uncomfortable with her answer.

She gave him a big hug.

"I'm tired so I think I'll hit the sack. See you in the morning."

"Sleep tight," he replied, sensing a vulnerable note in her voice, one that bothered him.

Chapter 11

Early the next morning, the constant ringing of David's phone woke him. He wiped the sleep from his eyes and picked it up. The voice on the other end surprised him.

"Wake up Sleepy Head," said Alesha. "Would you like some company?"

"Are you kidding? Of course I would," he answered. "But it's only 7 o'clock. On top of that, how do you plan to get here?"

"My mother brought me a brand new BMW."

David stretched, yawned, and sat up on the edge of his bed.

"That's one hell of a nice gift."

"Well, I want to see you and since my father is out of town, this is a perfect time to break it in. Where do you live?"

"This is crazy."

"Don't you like to do crazy things once in a while?"

"Well, ah—yeah, I guess so."

"Then tell me where you live?" she demanded, determined not to waste a single minute of her time with him.

"Sixty-two Washington Ave, Natick."

"See you shortly."

***

David slipped on his clothes and tiptoed to the front door. Less than ten minutes later, a blue convertible BMW crept up the driveway and came to a stop.

As soon as he opened the front door, her arms embraced him and their lips met with warm enthusiasm.

She looked gorgeous, dressed casually in a brown wool-lined leather jacket, blue oversized turtleneck sweater, black slacks and leather and glitter fabric boots. Her hair was hidden beneath a wool knit cap and worn in an easy style that required little care.

"I can't tell you how glad I am to see you," she said.

"My mother is still sleeping, so keep your voice down, OK?"

"Whoops, sorry," she whispered, slipping off her jacket and sinking down on the couch. "Are you glad to see me?"

"Yeah, I am, but not this early. And especially when I have to play in the All Star game this afternoon."

"So what's more important, a stupid football game or me?"

"The game," he replied, with a straight face.

She pushed him away, folded her arms and glared at him.

"You'd better be kidding, because if you're not, I'm out of here. And it'll be a long time before you'll see me again."

He gave her a barely perceptible smile.

"Of course, I'm kidding. Now sit back and relax while I cook us some breakfast."

"I'll help," she said, springing up from the couch and walking over to the Frigidaire©. "This is a nice, cozy place. How long have you lived here?"

"For as long as I can remember. So, what have you been doing since I last saw you?"

"Same old stuff, and thinking about you."

"That goes both ways," he replied, fiddling with the settings on the coffee machine.

Their conversation was suddenly interrupted by his mother's voice.

"David, are you talking to someone, or do you have the TV on?"

"I'm sorry if I woke you, but a friend of mine dropped by to see me."

"Is he playing in the game this afternoon?"

"It's not a he—it's a she."

"Oh," she said, her voice registering a bit of a surprise. "I'll be right there."

A few seconds later, she entered the kitchen. Her eyes took in Alesha and she threw her son a questioning look.

"So, my dear, how long have you known this *lovely* young lady?"

"For about two months now. I'm sorry that I didn't tell you about her sooner. Her name's Alesha."

To his surprise and delight, they instantly bonded with each other.

"And mine's Jane," she said, shaking Alesha's hand. "Do you like to cook?"

"I can do a nice fluffy cheese omelet."

"Good. Then grab an apron from behind the door and *fluff* up some eggs while I set the table."

The morning passed quickly. During that time, Jane Furie didn't ask very many questions about Alesha's family background. She seemed to have more important things on her mind, like the man she met just a few weeks ago.

Chapter 12

Bill Parham liked to go dancing on the weekend. He was an excellent dancer—strong, sure and fluid. When he was on the dance floor, he tried to imitate his favorite dancer, Fred Astaire, known for his energetic and athletic dancing style.

While he impressed people with his moves, he also impressed them with his attitude. He had this funny, prissy, sophisticated way of talking—using big words when he didn't have to.

The only person he didn't impress was David. So when Jayne Furie finally invited him to dinner, David paused before him, resisting the instinct to stick out his hand for a handshake.

It simply wasn't like him to be rude like that, she thought, sensing a chill in the air.

"David, would you mind pouring us a glass of wine—supper will be ready in ten minutes. That'll give you guys a little time to get to know each other better," she suggested.

"Perfect, because I have to be out of here in an hour so I can meet Chris. We're going to the movies."

After she returned to the kitchen, Bill attempted small talk, but the tension was palpable.

"Your mother tells me that you're quite a football player," he said, sitting back with his glass of wine. He smelled the contents, frowned and took a sip.

"She tells everyone that."

"I don't think she'd say it if it wasn't true."

"Let's just say that I was lucky to be on a team that had lots of really good players on it."

"I find football a little boring to watch, but I bet it's a blast to play."

"So, what's your favorite sport?"

"Golf—would you like to try it someday?"

"Thanks, but my college entrance exams are taking up a lot of my time."

"I'm glad Scots lived in Scotland for centuries."

"Why is that?"

"If it hadn't been for white folks, golf would have never been invented. Blacks just don't have enough brain power," Bill said unconsciously.

If his comment was meant to be a joke, it didn't sit well with David. Fortunately, his mother interceded.

"David, show Mr. Parham your scrapbook—the one with all of your football pictures in it."

He didn't say a word. He just did as he was told.

The conversation at supper was not about football or movies, but focused more on the subjects Bill liked best—ballroom dancing, golf and sports betting.

***

Born and raised in Providence, R.I., he dropped out of high school shortly after turning fifteen and became a grifter.

It wasn't a very profitable venture because he had to split the take with two other people. Seldom, if ever, did he have much to show for his efforts.

His smooth talking ability caught the attention of mafia boss, Freddy (The Fox) Giansolo, who taught him everything he knew about the numbers game and how to memorize number combinations.

Parham was crazy about his job. All he did was drive through poor and working-class neighborhoods and collect bets and cash from gamblers that he turned over to an illegal betting parlor.

In the evening, he'd make the rounds again to deliver the cash winnings to the parlors whose customers had hit the winning number.

Aspiring to become a 'made man' he sometimes worked around the clock collecting bets in nightclubs, liquor stores, bars and beauty shops.

His determination and tireless effort impressed Giansolo, who put him in charge of the *Jones market* an illegal betting operation in Boston's black community with profits of up to $10,000 a week.

***

July 1997: Parham's dream ended when a grand jury in the trial of 71 defendants charged that ten policy houses had been paying $2,000 a month in bribes to the chief of police, the head prosecutor and several city officials. Smaller bribes went to police sergeants and lieutenants.

August 2009: After several car bombing, one in which Giansolo was killed, Parham, thinking he'd be next, quickly left Boston for a long vacation.

Hidden at the bottom of his suitcase was $20,000 that he was going to hand over to Giansolo. He stashed away an additional $20,000 in a locker at the Framingham Bus Depot.

As long as all that cash is available, why not use some of it to get the hell out of town until things cool down.

The Sunny Bay Hotel and Casino in Guayanilla, Puerto Rico was his next stop. It was close enough to many of the country's most popular attractions and proved for a while to be a perfect hideout.

Locally owned and managed, it had undergone some costly improvements over recent years. It was an attempt by the owner to expand the tourism industry on the southern part of the island.

The two bars, one surrounding the swimming pool, were prime rendezvous spots, just like any place with a television set that could show closed-circuit international soccer.

After checking out his new surroundings, he introduced himself to the owner at a welcoming party in the hotel's undersized reception room.

His name was Rolly Gutierrez, a bald, naïve middle-aged guy with a bushy beard and a paunch like a kangaroo.

Parham used his smooth way of talking in an effort to convince Rolly that having a couple of prostitutes around would help stimulate business.

Rolly didn't like the idea.

"I'm sorry, Senór," he said. "But if the Gaming Division ever found out that there were prostitutes working here, they'd take away my license. And I can't afford to let that happen."

It didn't look like he was ever going to change his mind. So Parham decided to play another mafia style underhanded trick on him.

"Listen, I know you're eventually going to need some extra cash to upgrade this place. So here's a little something to help with the renovations," he said, sliding an envelope with $10,000 in it across Rolly's desk.

"That'll take some of the pressure off of you, so you don't have to worry," he added.

"What do you want in return?"

"You manage the hotel; I'll manage the casino. You get twenty percent of whatever the casino takes in. Everything else is mine. Got it?"

Rolly looked at the envelope wide-eyed, then back at Parham.

"Make it twenty-five and you've got a deal."

"Done," said Parham, reaching across Rolly's desk and shaking his hand. "Draw up an agreement."

Rolly had a worried look on his face.

"Please don't mention this to anyone, including my wife."

"No problem. If she ever figures out what's going on, I'll explain everything to her. Partners—remember?"

There's one important thing that Rolly failed to realize. Nowhere in their agreement was she mentioned. And when you go into any kind of business, it pays to pick your partners carefully.

***

Rose Gutierrez, a former singer and Puerto Rican beauty queen, arrived on the beach at the same time as Bill Parham, by pure coincidence.

He was seated comfortably in a lounge chair checking out the Hialeah Race Track Results when, from a short distance away, she dropped a towel on the sand and began her daily ritual.

Her streaky blonde hair and skimpy black and white bikini exaggerated her extraordinarily beautiful face.

Small-boned, shapely and slender, her eyes were masked by sunglasses, the frames shaped like hearts.

She began applying sun-tan lotion to her already tanned body. Then she sprayed herself with water from a plastic bottle.

Next, she pushed the straps of her bikini down toward her waist, exposing her breasts.

She looked up quickly, peered over the top of her sunglasses and caught him staring at her.

The only thing he could think about was the movie, Dr. No, in which Ursula Andress emerged from the water and walked toward Sean Connery in a flimsy two-piece swimsuit.

For a minute or two, that unforgettable scene jumped backward and forwards in time; she was Ursula Andress and he was Sean Connery.

Meeting her was positively surreal!

They exchanged smiles and Parham thought this would be a good time to introduce himself.

"Hi there, my name's Bill Parham and please excuse me for staring," he said. "But in all of my travels, I've never met anyone as lovely as you."

She held out her hand where a huge diamond ring glittered on her ring finger.

"Mine's Rose, and thanks for the compliment," she replied. "Puerto Rico is full of beautiful women, so I assume you haven't been here very long."

"About a week and might I add that it has been absolutely wonderful," he answered with a salacious grin.

"Are you staying at this hotel or did you just drop by for breakfast on the patio?"

"I've been here about a week. What about you?"

"I'm part owner. But I don't do much of anything except make sure the entire place is clean before guests arrive. My husband does everything else, like bookkeeping and renovations."

Good. She doesn't know that I gave him some cash to get those renovations started.

He wanted to look cool and calm so he took a long drag from his cigarette and blew out a puff of smoke.

"I think I met your husband when I first got here."

"My husband—I think you mean 'El Canarinho Grandé'."

"I'm sorry, but I don't speak Spanish."

She looked at him with a devilish grin. "It means the large canary because he's always chirping, always complaining about something."

"Like what?"

"Business and how he wants to fix this place up. I wish he were more romantic."

"If it was me," he joked, "I'd make your wish come true."

She laughed and said something in Spanish, "La vida horizontal haría que este lugar se cayera."

"Too much horizontal living would cause this place to shake and fall down."

She shivered as his lips parted in a smile, revealing two even rows of sparkling white teeth. "Maybe someday, when you're not so busy, you can teach me some Spanish."

"Maybe," she replied.

There was charm in her voice and soon they were chatting comfortably with each other.

She met her husband in Miami while selling her songs and singing in bars and lounges with a small band.

During her show business career, she competed in a personality and beauty contest and spent two months in a film studio as an extra.

"Did you get paid for your efforts?"

"Unless you win first place in a beauty contest, all you get is a cheap plastic trophy. Acting is a whole different story that's not even worth talking about."

"It sounds like a whole lot of people took advantage of you."

"They did. But it taught me a lesson."

"Like what?"

"Tough times never last, but tough people do," she answered, looking him straight in the eye. "That's why, when the time is right, I'm going to leave here and go back to Miami."

"I hope you don't leave too soon. If you do, I'll never get to know you."

"Don't worry, I'll be around for a while," she replied, glancing at her watch. "Listen, I've gotta go. If you're here tomorrow, we'll talk some more, OK?"

"I'd love too."

She slipped the straps of her bikini back over her shoulders, gathered up her belongings and wiggled her fingers at him.

"Have a pleasant stay. Maybe I'll see you this evening at our sunset cocktail hour."

"I'll be there."

Chapter 13

Rose could always be counted on by her husband to provide information and friendly conversation at what she considered *boring cocktail hour receptions.*

Although both were blessed with the ability to get things done, she was able to read in the looks and salutations of everyone she met what they thought of the hotel. And she used her beauty to her advantage.

She glided onto the patio floor in hot red culottes, a multi-colored blouse with a plunging neckline and white high heels. Her gold watch flashed, her gold earrings did, too.

The scent of her perfume was so strong, one honeymooner almost choked on his Sangria as she passed by.

It's a good thing his wife was talking to some guests or his honeymoon would have ended right there.

Parham wasn't at all surprised by the man's reaction. It was Rose's time to show off her captivating beauty and she did it with ease. This was her stage and she wasn't about to share it with anyone.

He was sitting alone at the far end of the bar when she approached and pointed at his drink.

"That cocktail looks pretty lethal," she said. "Another one of those and you'll fall off your chair."

"Well, there's an old saying, 'wherever an ass falleth may it never fall again'"

"You do have a way with words, don't you?"

He leaned forward with a sly smile. "Only if it gets me somewhere."

She smiled at him brightly. "Gilipollas (asshole)."

"What does that mean?"

"It means *enjoy.*"

He tipped his glass up to his lips and took a small sip. "I plan too. In fact, after I finish this drink, I'm going over to the casino to play a little blackjack."

"Good luck," she said. "See you on the beach tomorrow morning. Buénos notches, mi amigo. (Good night, my friend)"

Chapter 14

He spotted her the next morning lying on a lounge chair in a blue wet tank top, white rolled-up shorts and usual sunglasses, her braids cascading halfway down her back.

As he approached her, she struck a sexy pose and popped one leg in front of the other.

"Good morning," he said, waving his hand in her direction. "Looks like another great day."

"Buenos Dias," she said, "I see you brought your camera with you."

"It's a good thing to have when you're surrounded by so much beauty," he replied, eying her with lust. "On top of that, I'll be talking to a friend later today who has lots of show business connections. I bet he'd love to see some pictures of you."

"I've been told that many times before. And where did it get me?"

He shook his head.

"That's a tough question for me to answer. But I will tell you this. I'm serious about helping you get your movie career back on track."

"Before I'd consider doing anything like that, would your friend provide me with a legal contract that my lawyer could look at?"

He swallowed and choked back an honest reply.

"Ah—let's see how things go first. Now, how about me taking some nice pictures that I can send to him?"

"I hope you don't mind if I see them first."

"No problem," he said, motioning for her to move a little bit to her left so she'd be in the best spot for a great shot.

"How's this?" she asked, mussing up her hair and twirling around before cracking up.

"What's so funny?"

"I was just thinking about the first time I met my husband. He also wanted to take pictures of me. And I ended up marrying him. How ironic is that!"

"Would you still be with him if he didn't have lots of money?"

She shrugged her shoulders. "I don't know. He's a nice guy and I know he loves me. If there's something I want, he gets it for me."

Lucky lady, he thought, motioning to her to turn in different directions.

If her poses reminded him of someone, it was nothing compared to her face. Something about her eyes, with their alluring upward glance, mesmerized him.

She whirled around and pushed her hair from the back of her neck to the front of her forehead.

"How's this?" she asked, again.

"Thanks—I think that'll do," he said, placing the lens cap back on his camera.

She was hot and sweat dripped into her eyes. "I'm going to take a quick dip. Afterwards, we can go for a walk."

"I'll be waiting right here."

Following their walk, they felt exhilarated and decided to cool off beneath the shade of a small bluff overlooking the ocean.

"This is my own *little* private spot. When I want to be alone, I come here to meditate," she said.

"It'd be a great place for you to teach me some Spanish."

"I guess I could if you don't mind getting up at six in the morning, because I only have a couple of hours to spare."

"I'm an early riser, so I accept your offer," he quickly replied, his head stuffed with silly romantic thoughts.

"You don't waste any time, do you?"

"Someone once said that a waste of time is the most extravagant and costly of all expenses."

"That's exactly why I have to go and supervise my employees."

"Don't you ever get any time off?"

"Only when the season changes, or if I get sick, which is not very often," she answered, blessing herself.

"I really enjoyed being with you. Have a pleasant day."

"Qué pases un buen día, which also means have a good day! Gracias."

For a few seconds, he was frozen by the sight of her jogging back to the hotel, her shapely buttocks wiggling beneath those tight rolled-up shorts.

Chapter 15

It wasn't very hard for Rose to figure out what was going on in Bill Parham's head. She had been through it many times before, a stranger hitting on her with only one thing in mind: sex.

However, she liked him because even though she considered him to be a handsome and charming man, he didn't appear to be overly seductive. So their meetings at her *little* private spot on the beach continued.

Rose was an ardent Catholic and there were a number of times during her adult life where her religion saved her.

She didn't smoke, and she didn't believe in prostitution, drugs or gambling. However, she loved the cash that they brought in.

She had an excessive interest in clothes and spent an enormous amount of money on them.

After a busy day, she'd eat supper, return to her bedroom, take a shower and hit the sack. There was nothing more important to her than a nice relaxing beauty sleep.

She had no idea that a short step away, prostitutes were working inside the casino. And that Bill Parham was managing the place.

As soon as renovations were completed, business began to pick, up and more money began to flow in.

Early one morning, she awoke and found a brand new Mercedes Benz parked outside the hotel entrance. Resting on the front seat was a bouquet of red roses with a card that read:

Feliz cumpleaños (Happy Birthday)
Te Amo (I love you)
Rolly

When she told Parham about his generous gift, her voice throbbed with emotion.

For a moment, he felt something inside his body that he had never felt before; a slight touch of jealousy.

"That's a hell of a nice gift," he said, deciding not to say what he was thinking.

"He's been a different person since business picked up."

I wish I could tell her that part of the money came from the casino's earnings.

"I've got a good idea. Why don't we forget today's lesson so you can take me for a spin in your new car?"

"I guess I could. But I have to be back here in two hours because my husband and I are going to Ponce to celebrate my birthday with my in-laws."

"Happy Birthday. I hope this day is filled with smiles, sunshine, love and laughter."

"Gracias, mi amigo (thank you, my friend)."

"Da nada (no problem)," he replied.

She drove a short distance and stopped at a popular sightseeing spot where they enjoyed a spectacular view of Guayanilla Bay. Hills and mountains caressed the bay and glistened in all directions.

"I bet anyone who has been here will remember this place for a long time," he said, taking a few pictures of the bay before aiming his camera at her and taking a few more.

"How long do you plan to stay here?" she inquired.

"If I keep winning at the blackjack table, maybe a lot longer than expected."

Her next few words came as somewhat of a surprise. "I'm glad to hear that."

"If my luck runs out, and I had to leave tomorrow, would you miss me?"

"Of course I would," she answered, sadness showing in her eyes. "You've been very nice to me. So why don't we take a couple of selfies?"

"That's a good idea. If I had known that today was your birthday, I would've bought you a nice gift."

She moved closer to him.

"Just kiss me on the cheek and I'll consider that the nicest gift a guy could give to a girl."

He set the timer on his camera and had every intention of kissing her but the location of the car's stick shift presented a problem. So when he leaned forward, instead of kissing her cheek, their lips met.

She threw her arms around his neck and gave him a kiss that he'd long remember. After a couple of seconds, she pushed him away and apologized.

"I'm sorry—I'm sorry, I shouldn't have let that happen."

"It's not your fault," he said, settling back in his seat. "Anyone could get hooked on this place. It's perfect for romance."

She looked out over the bay. "Yes, it is."

"So don't be ashamed. What just happened could happen to anyone."

She glanced at her watch. "To make sure it doesn't happen again, I think we should go for a short walk before I drive you back to the hotel."

"Good idea," he replied, noticing how the ocean breeze made her dress move as if it was alive, and how her black hair swept across her features.

What he said next was the opposite of what he was thinking.

"I don't want to cause any problems between you and your husband, so why don't we cool it for a while?"

"Yes, maybe we should. But before we go, I want you to know that I've enjoyed every second that we've spent together."

"I hope that it's not our last."

"What will you do with all your spare time?"

"I think I'll take some dancing lessons."

She turned from him abruptly.

"Be careful of Puerto Rican dance instructors. They're all so charming and pretty you might fall in love with one."

He caressed her hair with a surprising gentleness. "Let me assure you that when I wake up in the morning, the only person I think about is you. And that's the god honest truth."

With each word that he spoke, she felt herself growing closer to him.

"I want to leave him. I want to be with you. I just can't yet," she replied.

The attraction between them was very strong. So strong, in fact, that in less than two weeks they were back together again on the beach where they became intimate friends, and close companions.

In his arms, with his warm breath on her cheek and the smell of his cologne surrounding them, it was for her an exciting experience.

Chapter 16

Most mornings in Puerto Rico don't begin with a chill in the air followed by intermittent rain. It's usually sunny and warm. When a heavy fog rolled in across the bay and engulfed everything in its path, half of the hotel's cleanup crew decided to stay home. Whenever that happened, Rolly had to pick up the slack.

Bill Parham was fast asleep when Rolly dispatched four of his employees to the casino to help clean up the place after a busy night.

They consisted mostly of family members who were faithful in word and deed. So when one of them found an unlocked storage cabinet filled with boxes of prophylactics and sexual lubricants, a red light went on.

Not only did the sight of them infuriate him, he felt like he had been betrayed. And he suspected that his wife and Parham knew something about the storage cabinet and what was hidden inside.

He summoned her to his office and slammed a box of prophylactics down on his desk. "What the hell are these doing in the casino?" he asked, his voice quivering with anger.

She tried to speak calmly while answering but it was impossible. "I'm sure it—it was Bill Parham's idea."

Suddenly, he felt dizzy and nauseated. "What the hell are you talking about?"

She glanced at her watch and back at him.

"Don't you two usually meet here so you can split up the night's take?"

He sat back in his chair and stared at her in disbelief, shaking his head.

"Yeah, and he'd better have a good explanation."

A few minutes later, the office door swung open.

Upon entering, the first person Parham saw was Rose, a very dim and disturbed look on her face. *Something is going on, or she wouldn't be here*, he thought.

Then he saw the box of prophylactics sitting on Rolly's desk. As he passed her, he noticed his eyes were fastened directly on him, and not in a friendly way.

"Good morning," he said, trying to make the atmosphere feel relaxed and inviting.

Rolly pointed at the box.

"There's nothing good about a morning when boxes of those, along with other nasty things, show up in the casino," he said angrily.

"Well, first let me say, that it was all my idea."

"And let me say that it was a bad one."

"Not really, if you consider the ten thousand dollars that I gave you to get renovations started around here. And what about that new car your wife is driving? Where do you think part of that cash came from?"

"Dirty money—illegal money—and you knew about it all the time?"

"Don't forget, it was you who let me manage the casino."

"Prostitution was never mentioned or even discussed in our agreement. If it had been, this would have never happened."

He reached into his desk draw and pulled out the agreement. Just when he began to tear it up, Rose reached across his desk and stopped him.

"Cariño, Señor Parham, has done a lot for us. Why don't we let things stay the way they are until the season changes?"

His face flushed and his eyes widened with anger. "No way and just to keep him from going back on his word, I want him out of here RIGHT NOW!"

He looked at her with an irritated glance as he ripped up the agreement and tossed the remnants into the wastebasket.

Parham shrugged his shoulders and extended his arms like it was no big deal.

"After we split up last night's take, I'll be out of here."

"All you're taking out of here are the clothes on your back and a one-way ticket to—to—wherever the hell you came from," Rolly said.

Parham looked at Rose with a convincing smile. "I thought you and I were *very close* friends. Don't you have anything else to say about this?"

For a second, Rolly stared at him, too stunned to move or speak.

"What do you mean?"

"She knows what I mean. Why don't you ask her about the good time we had on the beach while you were working?"

"No Señor Parham, I don't have to ask her anything," he said, pulling a snub nose revolver out of his draw. "I trust my wife. She would never do anything to hurt me."

"Whoa, be careful with that," Parham begged, raising his hands in front of his face to protect himself.

Rolly's next few words contained an implicit threat. "If you say anything else bad about my wife, I will shoot you. Do you understand? I *definitely* will shoot you."

"Yeah, yeah—I understand," he answered, slowly lowering his arms.

"Good," Rolly replied, placing the gun down on his desk. "I'll arrange a ride for you to the airport. If you hurry, you might catch the Delta 10:50 back to the states."

"Mind if I pack first?"

"While you were talking to my wife, I secured your room. As soon as we know where you are, we'll pack the rest of your belongings and send them to you."

"What about my split of the casino money?"

"We're going to keep that plus the ten thousand dollars that you gave to me. It'll help pay for your tab," he said, delighted by the look of surprise that crossed Bill's face.

There wasn't much more he could say so he left Puerto Rico with only one thought in mind. *I'm a dead man if I don't find a way to replace that money.*

***

For the next few months, he lived in a boarding house where he and Karl Toomey, a Natick, Mass, police officer, became good friends.

Toomey was best known around the area for organizing local *Back the Blue* events across New England.

He was reprimanded and placed on desk duty for six months after roughing up a black teenager suspected of shoplifting.

A racist and an outspoken critic of police reform, his mouth was as big as his bluster.

"Blacks, Jews, Asians, Chili eating mother fuckers—they're all alike," he preached. "If you're not careful, they'll take everything that you own away from you."

Soon he became Parham's mentor. And the more hatred that spewed out of his mouth, the more Parham began to believe he was right.

Immediately, he began to think about how Rolly Gutierrez sort of beat him at his own game.

That was an awful lot of hard earned cash that I was forced to leave in Puerto Rico and right now there's no way of getting it back. That is, unless I find a way to stay in touch with Rose.

Days of listening to Toomey's bitterness and discontent mixed with his hateful rhetoric eventually turned him into a perfect recruit for the American neo-Nazi Party.

Chapter 17
Present Day

The minute supper ended, David politely excused himself, slipped on his jacket and dashed out the door.

As the evening slowly wore on, his mood climbed to somewhere between a blue funk and resigned neutrality.

He walked into Wellman's with a disgruntled look on his face, a look that told Chris something was wrong.

"Hey dude, you look pissed off about something. What's up?"

"Nothing," he answered sharply, slumping down in a seat across from Chris.

"C'mon man. I've known you long enough to know when something's bugging you. Has it got anything to do with Alesha?"

Outside of his parents, the only person he ever felt comfortable talking to when it came to personal matters was Chris, so he relented.

"No, it's got nothing to do with her."

Chris snapped his fingers. "I know what it is. Your balls got caught in the zipper of your pants and you can't get them out."

David's expression brightened and he laughed at Chris's joke.

"The guy that my mother just met is a real dick."

Chris half smiled. "Why'd you say that?"

"During supper, he said a few things about minorities that I didn't like."

"Is that the only reason?"

"No," David replied, his mind wandering back to the racist remarks hurled at him and his teammates when they played games away from home.

"He strikes me as the kind of person who could stir up a lot of racial tension at a game. Like the one we played last year where we practically had to fight our way out of the stadium."

"You really think so?"

"Yes, I do."

"Why don't you let it go for now," Chris said, "Because sitting there fuming isn't going to get you anywhere; I've got some news that will."

"I could use some right now."

"Wellmans is catering for the Annual Judge's Dinner next Saturday at the Cross mansion."

"Is that something I should be happy about?"

"You will be after I tell you about this cool little plan that Jenny and I put together."

"I'm all ears," he replied, feeling less gloomy.

"A large crowd is expected to attend, so my father asked me if I had any football friends who'd like to help out. The first person I thought about was you."

"I don't know a single thing about serving food."

"You don't have to, because you'll be serving water."

"That's just great; I've gone from a football player to a water boy in less than a minute."

"It's the only way we could get you inside to see Alesha. All you have to do is smile every time you fill a glass with water. The ladies will appreciate that."

"That's pretty damned clever," he said, a flare of interest in his eyes.

"Check out the menu that my father put together," Chris said, sliding a copy across the table.

David read it aloud. "Oven roasted salmon with Chardonnay Truffle Emulsion, Simply Roasted Chicken, and Risotto with cauliflower and black truffles, coffee and dessert. Food for the rich and famous," he said with a slight snicker.

"Yeah—and when everyone's stuffed and the lights go down, that's when all eyes will be glued on the judge's table. That's when Alesha will excuse herself and meet you in the kitchen."

"I appreciate everything you and Jenny have done for me."

"No problem. Just remember, you'll only have ten minutes to talk to her before she has to get back to her table. That's when the speaker ends his BS and the judge addresses the crowd."

"That's just enough time for me to get in a couple of kisses."

"It might be a good idea to check out your surroundings before you do."

"I will," David reassured him.

Chapter 18
The Annual Judge's Dinner

Alesha could hardly wait for the lights to dim. When they did, she turned to her mother and excused herself; told her it was a *bathroom call*.

"Are you alright dear?" her mother whispered.

"Yes—yes, I'm fine," she answered. "My stomach's a little upset, that's all."

Her mother nodded understandingly and Alesha hurried off to the kitchen. In the background, she could hear the guest speaker begin his speech:

"From his appointment as a Boston Municipal Court Associate Justice to his current position, Judge Cross has contributed significantly in terms of his well-reasoned decisions plus his educational and administrative roles."

Listening to public speakers always made her nervous, but she usually got past their lengthy and boring speeches by picturing the audience members in their underwear.

She was dressed in a white silk gown with a V-neckline accentuated with a string of David Yurman crystal embellishments.

She topped that off with a Cartier watch, gold earrings, a necklace featuring yellow pearls, and an embellished silver clutch and white platforms.

Satisfied that no one was watching, she ducked inside the kitchen door. David was waiting and he wrapped his arms around her waist.

He tried to kiss her, but his lips just brushed her cheek.

"Honey, I'm sorry," she said, loosening his grip. "I want to kiss you, too. But if you mess up my makeup, my parents will know something's up."

"I understand," he said. "You know it's not easy seeing you standing there looking so lovely."

"That's so sweet. You look great, too."

"What have you been doing since I last saw you?"

"My college entrance exams and hanging out with Chris. What about you?"

"My tennis coach thinks I'm ready to play competitive tennis, and my parents think USTA Junior Tournaments are a great way to get out on the court and test my game."

"How do you feel about that?"

"Well, it'll give me a chance to learn and play against the best, and even make new friends along the way."

"Do you mean guys?"

"My parents would love me to meet someone who they'd approve of, but you've been in my heart from the very first day we met," she replied, pressing his hands against the center of her chest. "So you need not worry."

"I've received invitations from three different colleges to visit their campuses. Harvard is one of them."

"If you decide to go there, you'd still be close to me and perhaps we could see each other on the weekend and on holidays."

"Playing football and studying would be my first priorities, but we certainly could try."

"I want to see you as much as I can. So as soon as you decide, let me know," she said, glancing at her watch. "Now I've got to get back. And don't forget what I said."

"I won't," he replied, giving her hands a gentle squeeze.

She looked around again to make sure the coast was clear and stepped outside.

Standing in the shadows a few feet away was Karl Toomey, the very same cop who intercepted them nearly a month ago at Cochituate State Park.

He was on a protective team all hired by Judge Cross to protect the personal security of the attendees.

He focused his beady eyes on her. His broad shoulders were hunched forward and his chin jutted out as though the thoughts in his mind were not pleasant.

She looked familiar.

I've seen pictures of her on the judge's desk, so she's probably his daughter. But why would she be in the kitchen dressed like that?

He walked over to the kitchen door, slowly opened it and spotted David. It didn't take him long to put two and two together.

Dolley Madison, my ass. She's messing around with that black football player. The judge will be pissed when I tell him about this.

***

Alesha smiled at her mother to reassure her that everything was alright. Then she sat down, her attention totally focused on putting a stop to all distracting thoughts; the warmth of David's hands still resting on her chest. She found it difficult to sit there quietly and peacefully until the speaker introduced her father.

"—so without further ado, here is my friend, my mentor and my colleague, Judge Hermann Cross."

A hearty applause followed. Judge Cross flashed a wide smile, stood up, hugged the speaker, and shook his hand vigorously.

From deep within the recesses of her brain, she'd try to shut out her father's words, words that she considered empty rhetoric.

The following morning

During his 10 years on the police force, Toomey always felt that he was cut out to be a detective. He was everyone's image of a typical cop, a big white guy, six feet, two hundred-fifty pounds.

He liked being a cop, but he didn't like being assigned to public utilities, local government, real estate developers and entertainment venues.

Although they earned him some extra cash, he was tired of being stuck in a spot where there was no guarantee of promotion.

He often thought about his future on the police force. *After I tell the judge what his daughter has been doing behind his back, he might use his influence to get me a promotion to the detective squad permanently.*

A promotion would give him a certain degree of authority beyond police officers in specific situations, such as interrogation and use of force.

After Toomey told him what happened in the kitchen, Judge Cross was furious but his manner was somewhat restrained.

He didn't say much about Alesha's behavior even though his voice trembled nervously, and his hands shook uncontrollably.

He knew that she was easily influenced by her friends so he'd have to find another way to control her behavior.

His reputation would be tarnished if anyone ever found out that she was hanging out with people he did not approve of.

Toomey stood in front of him like an enlisted man hands folded behind his back, stiff and respectful.

"Are you positively sure that that football player was the guy she went back there to see?" the judge asked, his face stern and grim.

"They're the same couple that I saw parked in a car a couple of weeks ago at Cochituate State Park," Toomey answered.

"You're absolutely sure?"

"I wouldn't be here telling you this if I wasn't."

The judge gritted his teeth in silent fury before reaching into his desk draw and pulling out a bottle of Quinapril (heart medication).

He popped two tablets into his mouth and spoke in a commanding tone. "Don't mention this to anyone else, including my wife. Understand?"

"Yes, sir—ah—would you mind doing me a favor?"

"Don't worry," the judge said, waving his hand in front of Toomey's face. "I'll get you that promotion that you've been trying to get for the last few years."

"Thank you, sir."

"In the meantime, I need all the information that you can get on that football player; his name, his address and anything else that you can think of."

Chapter 19

As temperatures began to cool, the fall foliage all across the state glowed red and yellow in the morning sunlight. It was the kind of morning that Alesha decided to do something she rarely did; join her mother on the patio, eat a hearty breakfast and play a couple of sets of tennis.

"Good morning Mother," she said, with a big hug followed by a light kiss on the cheek.

It was an expression that Amanda Cross had not often seen and she was quick to take advantage of it. She looked up over the edge of her morning newspaper and greeted her with a warm smile.

"Good morning, dear. My, you're in a good mood today."

Alesha sat down and poured herself a hot cup of coffee.

"I slept great last night, better than I've slept in a long time. Beautiful day isn't it?"

"It certainly is. Have any plans?"

The radiant smile and the sparkle in Alesha's eyes were the clear signs of a woman in love.

"After my tennis lesson, I think I'll take Brutus for a walk. Then I'm going to study for next week's exams."

Her mother's eyes were very soft; there was a faint smile on her thin pink lips which gave the look of coldness, of reticence to her face.

"You're quite fond of that football player, aren't you?"

She sat back in her chair with a little yelp of surprise. "What football player?"

"Oh, come on Alesha. Don't pretend you don't know who I'm talking about," Amanda said. "I believe his name is David Furie."

"Who told you that?"

"This is a small town. Everyone talks. And if you know someone who has a nasty story to tell, they'll tell it. Apparently, someone told your father and he told me. At first, he was very upset, and he blamed me for not keeping a closer eye on you. I promised I would. But I also told him that you're old enough to pick your own friends. All he said in return was just remember, if you lie down with dogs, you'll wake up with fleas."

"That sounds just like something he'd say."

"I can understand his concern. Actually, I'm glad you have a boyfriend, as long as you're careful." She hesitated for a second before asking, "You have been careful, haven't you?"

Alesha frowned and her lips came together in a straight line.

"Yes Mother, I've been *very* careful. David is a really nice guy and he treats me with respect."

"Please don't take it personal darling. It's a question most parents ask their daughters when they reach your age."

The butler gave a little cough to announce his presence and Amanda Cross wiggled her fingers in his direction.

He approached and placed a fresh pitcher of orange juice and a plate of toast on the table.

"Will there be anything else, madam?" he asked.

"No, that's all for now," she answered.

Her sharp green eyes followed him as he left.

"You've got to be careful what you say around people," said Amanda. "I've always suspected him of spying on me and going back and telling your father about everything that I was doing."

"Why? Are you *doing* something that you shouldn't be doing?"

A slight smile crossed her thin lips. "Oh, I get it. Now it's your turn to grill me, huh?"

Alesha pursed her mouth in a self-satisfied smirk. "I think I'm old enough to ask you that kind of question."

Her mother's reply was somewhat ambiguous. "No, my dear, I'm not doing anything that I should be ashamed of. If I was, I'd do everything in my power to keep it away from him. He can be quite vicious at times."

Part of her answer was true, part of it wasn't. Their relationship had deteriorated to such an extent that she looked for the simplest excuse to get away from him. When he was out of town, she often spent her nights in the arms of Alesha's tennis coach.

Alesha suspected that something was going on between them, but she never broached the subject that had been playing on her mind for the last couple of years.

She gave her mother an understanding smile and laid her hand over hers.

"At times, there may have been some distance between us, but I love you, Mom—I love you."

"I love you too, darling. So you understand why it's important to present to the public the solid image that your father needs to someday get himself into a higher office. He has a good chance to make it, provided he keeps his record clean. That's all he cares about is his record. And that's why he's so concerned about you."

"He doesn't have to worry about me any longer. I promise that I won't do anything to tarnish his reputation."

Chapter 20

Professional football season was in full swing. It was a relief for David who, whenever Bill Parham arrived, would go over to Chris's house and watch the games with him.

He still couldn't accept the fact that another man, especially one that he didn't feel comfortable around, had entered his mother's life.

Sometimes he'd just lie in bed, eyes wide open, staring at the ceiling, waiting for his mother to come home. Even in the unnerving silence of his own bedroom, where he should have been comfortable, he did a lot of tossing and turning.

He noticed the changes that were taking place in her. She had changed her wardrobe, let her hair grow longer and didn't cook as often as she used to unless Bill Parham was coming for dinner.

The thought of going to college and only seeing his mother once or twice a month troubled him. He wondered if Parham's influence would change her life after he left.

***

Two weeks before Thanksgiving, he received an invitation from Harvard University to visit their campus.

Chris had already decided to attend Colby College in Waterville, Maine, on a football scholarship.

They often joked about their chances of playing against each other.

If it's true, that absence makes the heart grow fonder, every day that he was away from Alesha was tortuous.

She had no idea that her father had paid off her coach to see that she'd be on a number of Topnotch Tennis Tours over the next three months.

The tours organize and escorts tennis enthusiasts on luxury tennis vacations worldwide.

It would give her a chance to see the top professional players compete on the biggest stages.

David's occasional phone conversation with her didn't fill the emptiness that he felt in his heart while she was away.

The only person who seemed to be happy was Jane Furie. Parham's trusting smile and smooth, flattering words had melted her heart.

They went dancing almost every weekend except when he was either in Cambridge or Lowell, attending a neo-Nazi group gathering.

It didn't take long for emotions to bubble over. And when they did, David found himself in a place where he never expected to be.

He and Chris were watching the end of an exciting football game when Mr. Wellman, an intense look on his face, walked in.

Jacob Wellman was a rugged, sturdy and simple-hearted man of middle-age.

Born and raised in Bratislava, Czechoslovakia, his favorite hobby was studying Krav Maga, an Israeli martial art derived from a combination of various other martial arts such as boxing and Kung Fu.

After turning 15, his parents emigrated to Eilat, a busy Israeli port and popular resort where they opened a five-star restaurant.

When he wasn't working, he provided lessons on combat training to what would eventually become the Israeli Defense Force (IDF).

Following the Seven Days War between Israel and Egypt, his parents decided to emigrate again.

Next stop Natick, Mass., where he opened Wellman's Pharmacy and restaurant.

"Sorry to disturb you guys," he said, nodding his head for his son to leave the room, "but I have to talk to David about something very important."

"No problem," said Chris.

Now that they were alone, Mr. Wellman reached into his pocket and pulled out a piece of paper.

"Every four months, the accountant that your mother and I chose to run your family's insurance and investment business, audit the books. The last audit turned up something unusual."

"Like what?"

"There are a couple of withdrawals that your mother made over the past three months from one of the accounts."

"How much are you talking about?"

"Around ten thousand dollars; do you have any idea what she needed it for?"

"No, I don't."

"Chris told me that you were upset because your mother is dating a man that you don't feel comfortable around."

"If you don't mind, I'd rather not talk about *him*."

"We have to if we're going to find out why she gave Bill Parham all that money."

Mr. Wellman's words came as a complete surprise.

"You know his name?"

"Of course—it appears on all the checks that he cashed at the bank."

The muscles in David's face grew tight.

"When she first met him, he told her that he worked for a charity organization. Maybe that's why she gave him the money."

"Did he ever tell her the name of the organization?"

"I don't know."

In spite of himself, there arose a certain accent of suspicion in Mr. Wellman's voice.

"Please understand that I'm not the type of person who interferes in other people's business, but when this was brought to my attention, I felt I had to say something."

"I understand."

"Don't worry. I'll talk to your mother to see if she's aware of what Mr. Parham is *actually* doing with all that money."

"Thank you, sir."

Chapter 21

While driving home, David felt a spasm of panic sweeping over him. *Oh my god—my mother could be financially involved with a criminal.*

He was still much too young; too innocent to understand that when anger blinds the mind, truth disappears.

What upset him even more is when he pulled his car into the driveway, Bill Parham's car was parked in his spot.

All he could think about was Mr. Wellman's question, *Does your mother actually know what Mr. Parham is doing with all that money? How will my mother react when I ask her that same question?*

He could feel his heart pounding in his chest. And although there was a chill in the air, beads of sweat began to trickle down his back.

He swallowed back a tide of emotion and walked into the room where his mother and Mr. Parham were talking quietly.

She looked his way and smiled warmly. "Hi honey, did you enjoy the game?"

"I never got to see it all."

"Is everything OK—are you sick?"

"No—but you may be after I tell you what I found out today."

"If this is something that you'd like to talk to your mother about in private, I'd be glad to leave the room," said Parham, making a motion to rise.

He reconsidered it after David raised his hand and stopped him cold.

"What I have to say involves all three of us."

Jane could tell by the look on her son's face that something was troubling him deeply.

"What's wrong, honey?"

"Perhaps Mr. Parham wouldn't mind explaining what he did with all that money you gave to him."

His mother spoke first. "I donated it to his charity."

"Mom—please let him answer."

Parham fidgeted a moment and then began tapping his fingers on the arm of the sofa.

"Your mother already answered that question," he said.

"Would you mind telling us the name of the charity?"

"No—not at all; The Local Police and Justice Foundation."

"If that's the case, how come your name is the only one that appears on the back of those checks and you were the only person who cashed them?"

Parham looked at Jane and shrugged his shoulders because he didn't have a legitimate answer.

She wanted to scream at him; to demand an explanation, but understood how fruitless that would be and measured her best course to remain calm.

"I'm sorry Jane that I didn't tell you this sooner, but I had to use that money as collateral against some money that I *borrowed* a couple of months ago. I thought it would be the quickest way to pay it back."

She slumped back on the sofa. An expression of disappointment and betrayal overspread her charming face. She stared at him for a moment before she spoke.

"Part of this is my fault. I gave you the money because I trusted you and you deliberately lied to me."

Parham tried desperately to prevent his somber expression from matching one of a person walking the plank toward shark-infested waters.

"I'm sorry Jane, I'm really sorry. I thought I could resolve this matter before you found out."

David was too upset to be rational. And no matter how hard he tried, he couldn't contain his anger any longer.

"What do you take my mother for—a fool?"

"Calm down, son. I already apologized."

The hostility in David's voice and expression was unnerving.

"I'm not your goddamn son. So forget the apologies. All we want from you is the ten thousand dollars that you conned."

He drew himself up to his full height, glared at David and tried to push him aside.

"I'll have it back to you tomorrow, so move out of my fucking way so I can leave?"

"Running away from the truth, huh?" David said, retaliating with enough force to cause the Afghan rug to crumble and slide back beneath Parham's feet.

He stumbled and fell down, striking his temple on the edge of the coffee table.

There was an unnatural silence and then a scream.

It was his mother's voice.

"David! David! Stop!" she cried, grabbing his arm and pulling him away from Parham's lifeless body.

"He's faking, Mom—he's just looking for sympathy," said David. "I'll splash some cold water on his face and he'll be fine."

Jane bent over Parham and placed her hand over his heart. Then she felt his pulse. It was weak. A small rivulet of blood trickled out of his left ear and made three spots on his shirt.

"Cold water isn't going to help. He's in bad shape and we have to get him to the hospital."

"I hardly touched him, Mom. I hardly touched him."

"I know," she said, her calm expression hiding her inward panic.

"It was an accident. Now pick up the phone and dial 911. Tell the operator to get an ambulance over here, right away."

Chapter 22

It was a small headline in the morning newspaper, but it drew lots of attention. Before the day was over, it was the talk of the town.

An 18-year-old Natick man remains behind bars today after being arrested for assaulting another man during an altercation at his home.

According to police, 43-year-old Bill Parham remains hospitalized in critical condition after getting into an argument with David Furie, a popular Natick North High School football player.

The fight ended quickly when Furie allegedly pushed Parham and he fell, striking his head on a coffee table.

An investigation into the incident continues.

Amanda Cross's eyes were sparkling like a person who has a ton of good gossip to tell and is anxious to tell it.

But there was only so much she could say because she didn't want her daughter's name connected to David's.

While she drank her coffee and glanced nervously down the Metro section of the newspaper, she was glad Alesha was competing in a USTA Tournament in Arizona. She thought she'd have no access to any news back home.

As for Judge Cross, his delight could not have been greater than it was after he finished reading the story.

A smile tinged with racist thoughts flickered on his lips for an instant.

I've got that black bastard just where I want him and I'm going to make sure he never lays eyes on my daughter again.

***

David sat in a holding cell at police headquarters confused, upset, and scared. He was too shocked to give a detailed account of what actually happened.

The sickening stench of stale alcohol, stale smoke and an awful smell from the lavatories permeated the air.

He was exhausted, and just as his eyelids began to flutter someone's voice called out. "David Furie!"

"Yes, sir!" he answered.

A burly officer approached his cell and unlocked the door.

"You've just been bailed out. Sign the release papers, pick up your personal belongings at the front desk and you're free to go."

Waiting for him in a small reception room were his mother, Mr. Wellman and Chris.

He opened his arms, gave her a big hug and whispered in her ear.

"I'm so sorry that I took things into my own hands. I should have let Mr. Wellman handle it."

There was a sob in her throat, tears burned in her eyes. "I've been in a complete daze ever since this happened. But in a few minutes, you'll be out of here and I'm going to get you home and cook you a nice big breakfast."

"I must warn you," said Mr. Wellman, "that a bunch of reporters are outside waiting for a statement from you. Do not say anything. Understand?"

"Yes, sir."

"Let's go," said Chris, putting his arm around David's shoulder; in an attempt to shield him from the media.

***

Once they were home, Mr. Wellman explained that David's bail was nothing more than a conditional release with the promise that he'd appear in court when required. That, he said, would depend only on whether Bill Parham survived.

Meantime, Parham remained in a coma and was being kept alive by a life-support machine.

Every effort was made to track down his living relatives, but none could be found.

Puerto Rico, a month earlier: Rose Gutierrez's life became a living hell ever since the Casino incident. Her husband took away her car keys and kept a close eye on her.

No longer did she have the luxury of sun tanning on the beach, or going to bed as early as she used to. She felt that he was punishing her for something she was totally unaware of.

This is the fifth consecutive weekend that I've spent working and I'm fed up with it. The first chance I get, I'm out of here.

While packing Parham's few belongings, she found a locker key and his Minolta camera. She decided to wear the key on a chain hanging from around her neck.

It would serve as a constant reminder of how much her former friend and confidante's friendship meant to her.

***

Phoenix, Arizona: Alesha could hardly believe that she was competing in her final tournament of the fall. She had challenged herself playing in her toughest events and felt stronger and more confident about it.

The team she was on gelled and really pushed each other, which showed in their strong performances over the next couple of weeks.

They continued to be relentless in their daily habits and Alesha absolutely loved to compete. In tiebreakers, she cleared her mind and performed to her optimum ability.

She toured the country with her team, staying in plush hotels and dining in fine restaurants, all paid for by her father, who thought this was the best way to keep her away from David.

But the competition, no matter how tough, failed to take her mind off of how much she loved him.

It seemed inevitable that just when everything seemed to be going right, something would go wrong.

She was at lunch with her teammates when her phone rang. She took it from her pocket before the second ring. It was Jenny; her voice sounded shaky.

"Hi Jen, what's up?"

"Hi Alesha, I hope I caught you at the right time."

"You did. I'm at lunch. So what's going on back home?"

There was a slight pause before she answered. "I have some bad news?"

"What is it?"

"A story in today's *Boston Voice*. Hang on, I'll read it to you."

"A 43-year-old Natick man remains in a coma today following a fight during which he hit his head on a coffee table. According to the Norfolk district attorney's office, Bill Parham was confronted by David Furie at his Natick home on Washington Ave after Parham allegedly refused to discuss a fraudulent business transaction. Furie, 18 and a star football player at Natick North High School, planned to attend Harvard University next year."

Alesha felt light-headed and cold. She pressed her hand to her heart, tears welled up in her eyes.

"Oh no," she said. "Not David." Then she put her hand over her mouth before collapsing down in her chair, like a spring that had held her up had broken.

"Alesha! Alesha!" Jenny cried. But there was no answer.

When she regained consciousness, she could hear the subdued tones of several people outside of her private room at The Maricopa Medical Center.

Her throat was dry and she tried to sit up to reach for a glass of water. But all of her strength seemed to be gone. The glass slipped out of her fingers and crashed to the floor.

She flopped back on her pillow and within a second or two, a doctor and a nurse rushed to her bedside.

"What happened?" she asked.

"You fainted," the doctor answered. "Your coach applied CPR and kept you flat on your back until a medical team arrived."

"That has never happened to me before."

"When blood flow to the brain is short-circuited, whether the pressure is high or low, you can lose consciousness for a short while and faint. That's what happened to you."

"I see. How soon can I leave?"

"I talked to your father and he insisted that we keep you here until you feel better. He's flying to Phoenix tonight so he can see you."

Suddenly, she realized that she still hadn't got over the shock of what Jenny told her.

The doctor noticed tears gathering in her eyes, and he tried to console her with some encouraging words.

"I'm quite sure you'll feel better after you see your parents. Till then, I suggest you rest and try to relax while we fix you some breakfast."

Chapter 23

Alesha heard her door close, and the sound woke her from a light sleep. She squinted and put her hands up to her eyes to block out the sunlight that was streaming into her room.

Her eyes were puffy from crying herself to sleep and she could barely make out the blurred shape of her father seated nearby.

He stood up and approached her bed. As he bent over to kiss her, she noticed that he never looked as worried as he did right now.

"Good morning, my dear. How are you feeling?" he asked, grasping her hand.

"Lousy," she replied, withdrawing her hand and pointing it at the window. "Would you mind closing the curtain halfway?"

"Not at all," he answered with compassion. "Your mother was attending a fashion show in Montreal that's why she's a little late getting here. I talked to your doctor and he said that you could leave after he checks your vital signs."

She tried to say something but was unable to fight back her sobs.

"Whatever is troubling you; does it have anything to do with that black football player?" he asked.

"Everything," she answered bluntly.

"I thought so. Thank god you're not pregnant."

His indifferent coolness, and his air of superiority, aggravated her.

"Would it matter to you if I was?"

"Why, of course, it would. You seem to forget that you still live under my roof and as long as you do, you simply must abide by my rules."

"I have—every day of my life," she said, snatching several tissues from a box sitting on her night table and dabbing at her eyes. "But I'm not a child anymore so you might as well get used to the fact that I'm quite capable of picking my own friends."

Suddenly, it occurred to him that there might be another way to overcome the stalemate.

"You may not believe this, my dear, but I do love you. I may go away a lot, and at times I may not have been the best father, but I do care."

"You were so busy directing my life it never occurred to you that you were being disrespectful of me? What I needed and never got from you was your love and understanding. When you went away on those business trips, I really missed you. Then one day, I stopped missing you."

"I suppose that's when you met that black football player."

She nodded. "That's right—when I met David. He's kind and understanding and he listens to my problems. You never did, so what the hell did you expect?"

His face reddened. "Well, if he's so kind and understanding, why did he assault Mr. Parham?"

"All I know is what I heard and I don't believe *any* of it."

"So you plan to stick by him?"

"Yes."

All he did was make an absurd face and round his mouth like a fish out of water.

"Alright—have it your way. I promise not to interfere. But please be a little more discreet. I can't afford to have your name connected to his in any way."

He tried to kiss her but she turned her face away so he wouldn't see the tears in her eyes.

Feeling rejected, he patted her foot, stood up and buttoned his jacket.

"Get some rest. Your mother and I will be back later to see you."

Upon returning to Natick, the first thing he did was have Toomey visit him at his office.

He needed a strong plan, one that would preserve his reputation and keep Alesha and David apart, forever.

He picked the right person to set that plan in motion.

A look of extreme satisfaction crossed his face as he lit one of his favorite Havana cigars, propped his feet up on the edge of his desk and recline in his favorite chair.

Several days had gone by. And Toomey looked forward with eager anticipation to hearing what the judge had done, if anything, about his promotion.

"I've written a request to your boss to have you moved to the detective unit. All I have to do now is sign it and send it to him. In return, I want you to nail that black football player. Think you can do that?"

"Yes, sir. I worked out a plan that will definitely work."

"See that it does and you'll be a detective before the month is over."

Chapter 24

Three weeks passed before David received a summons to appear in court. During that time, an attorney hired by Mr. Wellman advised him not to talk to anyone about what happened at his house. That included Alesha.

He gathered as much information from David and his mother as possible to prove that what had occurred was a clear case of self-defense.

"It's considered to be a type of affirmative defense used to explain one person's use, of force against another person," he explained.

"For example, self-defense describes a situation where one person, in this case, David's, reasonably used force to defend himself against an attack by another person, Mr. Parham's."

"A person might use non-deadly force, or deadly force, to defend himself. If necessary, the use of deadly force can be permitted, depending on the circumstances. That's what we have to prove."

"How difficult is that?" Jane asked.

"It can go either way. And a lot depends on Mr. Parham's condition," he answered. "We'll just have to wait and see."

***

Another three weeks dragged by before the trial got underway amid a blaze of publicity.

Outside the courthouse, reporter's jockeyed for position, looking for tiny bits of information that would sensationalize the story.

Inside, more reporters scuffled for places upon the stationary benches that sat in the rear of the courtroom.

One investigative reporter had even dug up some information concerning Jane's alleged relationship with Parham using the bold headline: **Love Nest Trial Gets Underway.**

It was a rather ridiculous assumption, but it sold lots of newspapers.

Another reporter scribbled down what she had overheard, then added in brackets **Sensational** to attract her editor's attention.

The courtroom was packed.

David and his attorney were seated at a long oak wood table; to their left, the district attorney and his legal assistant.

Jane was seated directly behind them, a handkerchief knotted tightly around her fingers. Seated next to her were the Wellmans.

She usually had a smile on her face, but now she looked solemn.

Presiding over the case was Judge Charles Richardson, a colleague of Judge Cross.

The evidence the district attorney (DA) would present would be police photographs of Bill Parham sprawled out on the living room floor, a list of bank transactions, and testimony from the first officer to arrive on the scene, Karl Toomey.

After he was sworn in, the DA got off to a fast start.

"Would you please state your name and occupation?"

"Officer Karl Toomey—Natick Police Department."

"Would you please tell the court what you witnessed at eleven PM the night of November 13, two thousand fifteenth?"

"I received an emergency call to report to Sixty-two Washington Ave, Natick. Upon arrival, I found David Furie sitting on the front stairs of his house. He looked extremely worried and distressed."

The DA turned around and faced the crowded courtroom. "Is David Furie here in this courtroom?"

"Yes, sir."

"Would you please point him out?"

Toomey pointed at David. "That's him sitting over there."

"What did you find after entering his house?"

"Mr. Parham, unconscious; lying on the living room floor; blood coming out of his left ear."

The DA walked across the floor and stood in front of the jury. "What did you do after that?"

"I called for backup and an emergency medical team. We attempted to find out from Mr. Furie and his mother what happened. She said there was a misunderstanding and things got out of control. Mr. Parham tripped on a rug and fell, striking his head on the end table."

"When the backup arrived, did either one you search for any other evidence that might have led to Mr. Parham's injury?"

"Yes, sir, we did."

"Please tell the court what you found?"

"A half-gram of cocaine in Mr. Parham's pocket, along with two thousand dollars in cash and another half-gram of cocaine on top of the coffee table."

David and his mother jumped up at practically the same time.

"That's not true! That's simply not true!" she screamed.

And David shouted, "That's a lie. Nobody in our house uses drugs!"

Their objections were followed by a cacophony of protests from their supporters.

"Order in the court!" Judge Richardson shouted, banging his gavel down in an effort to restore order.

"If there are any more outbursts like that, I will be forced to clear the courtroom. Now I want everyone to calm down so we can proceed."

The DA waited several minutes before continuing. "How much is a half-gram of cocaine worth on the street?"

"Rough guess—around one-hundred thousand dollars."

"What is cocaine capable of doing to those who use it?"

"In addition to good feelings, cocaine can also cause irritability and paranoia. It can also cause death."

"So any student who might consider using it could die?"

"Objection!" shouted David's attorney. "The district attorney is leading the witness."

"Withdrawn," the DA countered sharply.

Judge Richardson leaned forward and spoke to the court stenographer.

"Strike the district attorneys' last question from the record. Proceed."

"Thank you, Officer Toomey," said the DA. "That'll be all."

Judge Richardson looked at David's attorney. "Do you wish to cross-examine Officer Toomey?"

"I have no questions for him at this time. But I'd like to reserve the right to question him later."

"Motion granted," he replied, making a note of his request on his court briefs. "Call the next witness."

The court clerk approached the judge's bench and read the name appearing on a witness statement form. "The state calls Glenn Ordway to the stand."

Ordway, a heavy set, fidgety man, came forward and was sworn in.

His tie was loose and he kept dabbing at the perspiration on his forehead with a handkerchief.

The DA looked at the sworn deposition that his legal assistant handed him.

"Mr. Ordway, what was your association with Bill Parham?"

He cleared his throat and answered, "I was his business partner."

"Did you ever see Mr. Parham and Mr. Furie together?"

He answered with a strong Boston accent, "Yeah—a couple of times."

"And where did you see them?"

"Cafés, restaurants, places like that."

"During these meetings, did they talk about selling drugs?"

"Sometimes they did."

"Would you describe these meetings as cordial?"

"Sometimes they'd get into arguments over how to split up the cash."

"Everything he's said so far is a lie," David whispered to his attorney.

The DA overheard David's words and gave him an intimidating stare. Then he looked back at Ordway.

"Do you recall the last time they got into an argument?"

"The day before Mr. Parham ended up in the hospital."

Unable to control himself any longer, David jumped to his feet.

"He's lying! Can't you see he's lying?"

"David, sit down!" his attorney pleaded, but to no avail.

Judge Richardson banged his gavel down several times and shouted. "Order in the court!"

"You lying sack of shit!" David yelled before hurtling the table. He grabbed Ordway's shirt and dragged him out of his chair.

Two court officers standing nearby reacted quickly. They rushed toward David, pulled him off of Ordway and locked his arms behind his back.

"Please don't hurt him!" Jane screamed her eyes wide with fright.

His best friend was in trouble and Chris felt an irresistible impulse to help him. He stood up, but his father restrained him. He placed his hand on Chris's shoulder and said, "Sit down! There's nothing you can do. Sit down!"

Judge Richardson banged his gavel down again. "Clear this courtroom immediately! Court is recessed until 2 o'clock. Both attorneys report to my chambers, NOW."

"You have a very hot-headed client there," Judge Richardson said to David's attorney. "His actions only lend credence to the DA's case. So I suggest that you two work out some sort of an agreement or I'll have to have Mr. Furie restrained until the end of the trial. That's something I don't want to do."

"That fellow, Ordway, is lying through his teeth," said David's attorney.

"He may be. But that's something that'll have to be proven. And we haven't heard from all the witnesses yet," replied Judge Richardson.

He exchanged his robe for a sports coat and hurried toward the door. "It's time for lunch. I'll see you back in the courtroom in two hours."

David's attorney took off his glasses and rubbed his tired eyes.

"I was thinking of calling Mrs. Furie to the stand. She's the only one who can unravel whatever was going on between the three of them."

"That's a tough decision."

"I know. I'm almost certain that my client doesn't want his mother's name linked to an alleged drug dealer. So he's ether sticking his neck out to protect her, or he wasn't doing anything illegal."

"Why would a kid with a clean record like his sell drugs?"

"That's a good question, one that the judge and jury will most likely consider after we've heard from all of the witnesses. Now, what do you say we grab a bite to eat while we still have a chance?"

An hour later, David, his mother, and their attorney met in a conference room and discussed the evidence the DA had presented.

"If you decide to plead guilty to the drug charge, I can file a *Motion to Dismiss* the assault and battery charge. Of the two cases, it's the weakest one."

It was an agonizing decision for David to make, but after everything that his mother had been through over the last few weeks, he didn't want her name plastered all over the paper.

"What's the worst thing that could happen?" he asked.

"Drug laws in Massachusetts are particularly harsh concerning drug trafficking and sale to minors or near a school zone, but less harsh for the federally illegal drug marijuana. Depending on what the judge has heard so far, he might be lenient and hand down a three to five-year sentence. Or he could suspend the sentence and place you on long parole."

"Is there any chance of that happening?"

"I've already talked to the DA. He said if you decide to plead guilty, he'll request a lighter sentence for you."

David saw tears rush to his mother's eyes, so he opened his arms and gave her a big hug.

"I'm sorry all of this happened. I only wanted to protect you and I guess I made a terrible mistake. I don't want you up there on the stand. So please don't worry, I can take whatever punishment I get."

When the trial resumed, he took his attorney's advice and had him file a *Motion to Dismiss* the assault and battery charge.

Judge Richardson approved the request.

In doing so, he stated, "Once someone uses excessive force, which is more force than the situation truly calls for, then he gives up his right of self-defense. Evidence presented so far by the district attorney indicates that David Furie was the person defending himself and Bill Parham the aggressor in the action."

"However, this trial will continue since nothing said thus far eradicates the testimony or the evidence presented earlier by the district attorney's office. This information is at the very heart of whether probable cause exists for bringing drug possession charges against Mr. Furie," he said, adding, "His constitutional rights require answers to these questions."

The first person to speak was David's attorney. "Your honor," he said, "the evidence presented in the drug case against Mr. Furie before court was adjourned appears to be extremely strong. Therefore, he wishes to change his plea from not guilty to guilty."

A sudden hush fell over the courtroom.

David was immediately placed under oath, and Judge Richardson questioned him to make sure he understood the charges, the possible penalties, and his trial-related rights.

"There are very few people in this courtroom who do not know you or like you," he said. "I'm positive they're all aware of your behavior, both on and off the football field. But those closest to this case also realize that you must pay your debt to society. The total amount of drugs found in your possession at the time of your arrest, and since this is your first time being arrested, the length of the sentence on average is typically around two to four years. You understand that?"

"Yes sir, I do," David answered.

"Then I shall proceed to the sentencing phase. During earlier court proceedings, it was never determined whether the drugs seized in this case were for personal use or for distribution of controlled substances. There were no dangerous weapons involved in their distribution. In addition, there was no proof that Mr. Furie distributed drugs that involved minors, or occurred near a school zone. However, earlier testimony provided by several credible witnesses proves, beyond a doubt, that drugs were found at Mr. Furie's home, and he has changed his plea from not guilty to guilty to having possessed them."

He glanced down at a desk calendar resting near his elbow and addressed both attorneys.

"Gentlemen, I have scheduled a sentence hearing for this Friday at ten o'clock. Is that acceptable to both of you?"

"Yes, your honor," they answered.

"Good. Then you both understand that no judgment will be entered into court records until it is reduced to writing, signed by me and filed with the clerk of court. This will help spare this town of a lengthy and costly courtroom battle."

"Yes, your honor," they repeated.

He banged his gavel down twice. "Good, court is adjourned until Friday at 10 o'clock."

Jenny and Alesha, who had disguised herself by wearing sunglasses and a blonde wig, were seated in the back of the courtroom.

Alesha's first instinct was to run over to David and tell him how much she loved him. But Jenny noticed tears flooding her eyes and grabbed her arm. "C'mon—Let's get the hell out of here before your face ends up on the evening news."

Chapter 25

A buzz of tension filled the air when Judge Richardson walked into the crowded courtroom and sat down behind the bench.

"Good morning. Before I proceed with the sentencing phase of this trial, I want everyone in this courtroom to know that I prepared a pre-sentence report that helped me decide the appropriate sentence for the defendant."

"The defendant has been given an opportunity to make any objections to this report and has chosen not to do so."

"The factors I'm considering before imposing a sentence provide satisfaction that the offender has been punished as well as sufficient rehabilitative factors that will prevent him from committing the crime again."

"After reviewing all of the aforementioned testimony, I must also acknowledge that the sentence I am about to hand down is considered the *lower end* of time typically handed to defendants in drug cases such as this. David Furie, please stand."

He obeyed and was followed by his lawyer.

"You understand the charges against you?"

"Yes, sir," David answered.

"The peculiar circumstances of this case justify, under the law, that I sentence you to two and a half years in prison, to be served at the Danbury Correctional Institute, Danbury, Connecticut, followed by six months' probation. Is there any statement that you wish to make to this court?"

"No, sir," David replied, his voice softened by emotion.

Jane Furie uttered a little moaning cry, reached over the courtroom railing and hugged and kissed him.

"Don't worry, Mom. I'll be fine," he said, quickly kissing her on the cheek.

David's attorney placed a comforting hand on his shoulder. "I'll do everything in my power to get you a new trial."

He looked around and spotted Jenny. There was no doubt that the person seated next to her in the blond wig and oversized sunglasses was Alesha.

He puckered his lips and blew a kiss in her direction before a court officer slipped a pair of handcuffs on his wrists and led him out of the courtroom.

Soon after, every reporter hurried out of the court to file their report.

Chapter 26
The Sunny Bay Hotel and Casino in Guayanilla, Sunday, 5:00 AM

Rose Gutierrez was busy supervising her cleanup crew when she spotted a small story in a discarded copy of the *Boston Voice*. "Bill Parham—Dios Mio," she said aloud, drawing the attention of one of her employees.

She knew that after a long busy night, her husband would still be asleep. And deep down in her heart, Bill Parham still meant something to her.

This might be her only chance to leave Puerto Rico.

She rushed back to the office where she always kept a change of clothing and put on a quick dab of lipstick. The only sound was the quiet whir of an electric clock that nurtured her thoughts.

"Money—I need money," she muttered, focusing her attention on the office safe. She knew the combination, but she had to hurry.

She bit her lip nervously and turned the dial, "I hope this is the right—10, 27, 33, 44."

Click, the door opened and she found what she was looking for, ten thousand dollars and a credit card that he had taken away from her.

She stuffed everything into her pocketbook, made sure she wasn't seen, and slipped out the hotel's rear entrance.

At that time of morning, with a little luck, she'd grab a cab to take her to the airport where she could catch Delta 8:20.

Destination: Miami International Airport with a connecting flight to Boston.

Chapter 27

Seagulls glided over the treetops surrounding nearby Candlewood Lake, their pale feathers shining against the azure blue sky.

Pigeons hovered over an immaculately landscaped courtyard, their eyes searching for crumbs. It was lunchtime at the federal prison at Danbury.

With its art déco-style front surrounded by 348 acres of rolling hills, it looked more like a country club than a prison.

Seventy-five percent of the inmates resided in one of eight large rooms, each divided by a tight configuration of cubicle partitions, making the rooms resemble an overcrowded office.

The cubicle that David shared with another inmate contained two bunk beds and lockers.

Despite missing his mother, Alesha and all of his close friends, he seemed to fit in comfortably with the prison's surroundings.

After reviewing David's intake report, the warden assigned him to the Recreation Department and granted him four hours of visiting time per month to discuss legal matters with his attorney.

Determined to make his time there as comfortable as possible, every morning he put on a sweat suit and jogged around the courtyard.

During the evening, he whiled away his hours reading, writing letters or taking college correspondence courses.

Ironically, the warden, much like David's father, loved football and knew of his father's heroics on the gridiron. While at Bates College in Lewiston, Maine, he thought he played against him.

David trusted his lawyer and felt he'd get him a new trial as soon as possible. However, things didn't quite turn out that way.

Six months after his incarceration, he received some devastating news that turned his whole world upside down.

One early June morning, he was summoned to the warden's office. On his way there, he thought his lawyer would welcome him with some good news. Instead, Mr. Wellman's presence told him that something was drastically wrong. He looked very intense as he stood up, advanced a step and gave David a fatherly hug.

"I apologize for not being able to share much better news with you today," he said, "so it might be a good idea to sit down before I do."

"Did Chris get hurt playing football?"

"No, he's fine. This is about your mother."

Mr. Wellman's words exploded in David's ears, his face to give way to one of despair.

"She has cervical cancer."

For a moment, he just stared at Mr. Wellman, too stunned to move or speak.

"So what's the prognosis?"

"She didn't want you to know, but she's been in and out of the hospital for the past two months. My wife and I talked to her doctor and—uh," he choked on his words, "uh—he said she has less than two months to live."

David dropped his head back and stared up at the ceiling, trying to hold back the onrush of tears.

He hardly ever cried, but intense emotion painted his expression. *This is the worst thing that's ever happened to me.*

With his sorrow, came anger and then, for some unknown reason, he quickly recovered his composure. He needed something, or somebody, to calm his mind. What would he not give for the sight of Alesha's kind face now, and a touch of her strong, comforting hand?

The warden's compassionate eyes caught the sorrowful look on David's face and he slid a box of tissues across his desk.

"Listen, son—when you're in prison and you get bad news like this, it's devastating. Not only are you nowhere near your friends and family when you're locked up, but you don't have your support system around you. Under the prison's honor system, I've made arrangements for you to be released today in the custody of Mr. Wellman. He'll help your lawyer put your family's business affairs in order."

He felt a lump in his throat, and tears begin to run down his cheeks. "Thank you, sir."

Mr. Wellman bowed his head in sorrow and silence. He knew David like he knew his own son. And he was aware of the problems that he'd encounter following his temporary release from prison. He swore that he'd protect him emotionally while remaining as supportive as possible.

David felt that his life would never be the same. A great and terrible sorrow had entered his life; he had lost his father, now he was about to lose his mother. And that began to weigh heavily on his mind.

We had a nice house. I had a car. I had a college scholarship. Everything has been taken away from me; my dad, and now my mom. Everything was going so well, and now I don't have much of anything. After all those years of taking good care of myself; playing football, exercising—my life has turned into a big lump of shit.

A steady diet of encouragement from the Wellman's would be necessary in order to help him find a new 'normal' in his life.

When he finally saw his mother, he was shocked by her appearance. Her eyes were sunken, her cheeks had fallen in, and a yellowish pallor gave her the look of a person suffering from a serious illness.

She had grown so thin and so weak that she practically had to be carried to bed.

Seeing her in such poor condition caused David's facade of normality to deteriorate. All he could think about was getting even with the people who, during his trial, deliberately lied.

Alesha didn't waste any time offering her support. She rushed over to his house, and the minute she saw him, she wrapped her arms around his neck and they cried together.

She noticed as she had not noticed before a streak of gray in his hair and a pathetic, weary look that haunted his eyes.

They didn't know how long they sat there and cried, but gradually their sobs subsided.

"Without my parents, I feel like I'm walking into another world," he said, "one that I don't recognize anymore."

A look of pure hatred flashed across his face. "All I think about is getting even with the people who lied at my trial."

"I know, but now is not the time to be thinking about things like that," she said. "Your mother needs all the support she can get. So you've got to be strong—everyone around her has got to be strong. Do you understand?"

"Yeah—I'll work on it. It's just that these first few days have been the hardest. I only did a year but every time I see a police car go by, even though I'm not breaking any law, my heart skips a beat. I wish I never had to think about why I went to jail again. I just want to put it all behind me."

"I think the best solution for what you're going through right now is hard work. I'll help you with that. I just want you to know that no matter where you are, I'll always be the person who is most concerned about you."

She said no more. The time had arrived for mourning and lamentation.

But over the next few days, new thoughts, some good, some bad, entered his mind.

The good thoughts allowed him to comport himself with great dignity at his mother's funeral.

He was somewhat bewildered by the whirl of bad thoughts that rushed through his mind: *I'll find the people responsible for my imprisonment and beat the shit out of them until they tell the truth. Make them wish they had never been born.*

During the repast, however, mourners talked, bonded and shared so many feelings and stories about Jane Furie and what a wonderful person she was, his pain subsided, replaced by spiritual warmth.

Because the Wellmans were so close to David's parents, they insisted that after his incarceration, he come, and live with them.

He gratefully accepted their offer.

After his furlough ended, Mr. Wellman drove him back to Danbury where he became withdrawn and pensive, hardly speaking to anyone.

He spent most of his spare time working out in the gym. Over the next few months, he transformed himself into a six foot, two inch two hundred twenty pound behemoth.

Chapter 28

David was in for a big surprise the next time he was summoned to the warden's office. Along with Mr. Wellman, his lawyer was also there. They both welcomed him with wide smiles and warm handshakes. They were somewhat surprised to see the physical changes in his body; that of a man used to muscular exercise, strong and wiry.

His long, sleek hair was tied in a tight braid. And despite the cold and wind, he wore only a long-sleeved sweater that hugged the muscles of his arms and shoulders beneath a down vest.

His face had lost its boyhood innocence and had grown rugged, as if perpetually crinkled in thought. His eyes were moist, pleading but suspicious as well.

"I'm glad to see you again," his lawyer said. "I apologize for not getting back to you sooner. But I finally have some good news."

"Right now, I could use some," David replied.

"Call it luck, but a couple of months ago, a woman who identified herself as Rose Gutierrez visited our office. She said she was a close friend of Bill Parham's, and that she's been following your case on TV and in the newspaper very closely. At first, I thought she was a model looking for a little publicity until she showed me a couple of pictures of them together. Those pictures proved that she was telling the truth."

"Why'd it take so long for her to come forward?"

"She feared that her husband, who she described as a violent man, might come after her so she decided to lay low for a while. Chances were slim that anyone other than her would have come along to prove your innocence and there she was, sitting right there in front of me. I asked her one important question, had she ever seen drugs in Mr. Parham's possession or had he ever mentioned selling them or using them? She answered, *never*."

David was almost speechless with anger.

"So instead of spending all this time in prison because of the lies those two assholes told, I could have spent taking care of my mother."

"I've been a lawyer for a long time, and over the years, I learned never to go back into the courtroom with just one witness. The next day I flew to Puerto Rico. I went to the Sunny Bay Hotel and Casino in Guayanilla. I asked several of her former employees the same question. And I got the same answer. Most importantly, I have sworn affidavits from all of them."

"Where do we go from here?"

"During your trial, there were a lot of sworn statements made by Officer Toomey and Mr. Ordway. I wouldn't say they were statements of facts but downright perjury. I've already requested a new trial for you. I'm optimistic that the outcome will be much different."

"I certainly hope so," he replied.

Natick District Court—one month later

Though he spoke softly, his lawyer's voice resonated throughout the courtroom.

"Three officers responded to the Furie residence; two produced reports within two days, and neither of them mentions finding drugs. Their body cams showed they also searched the garbage, but the video does not indicate they found anything."

"During a hearing at the Natick Police Department the officers denied three times that they found any drugs in or around Mr. Parham's body. Although Officer Toomey claimed that the drugs were found before their arrival, the affidavit for the search warrant does not mention the finding of any drugs."

The judge held up his hand and interrupted him. "You've mentioned Officer Toomey's name several times in your report. Are the other officer's names available?"

"They are, your honor," he replied, handing a copy of their names to the judge. "But they've requested they be kept private because the Natick Police Department is conducting an internal investigation focusing on the drug charges brought against Mr. Furie. In addition, the information I presented here today was not available during his trial."

"You've answered the question. You may proceed."

"Thank you," he replied. "Another officer photographed the Furie residence after the arrival of the search warrant. He photographed all the evidence, but again, there was no photograph of drugs. The first mention of cocaine did not occur in any of the paperwork until Officer Karl Toomey filed a supplemental report on October 19th as he prepared the arrest warrant for David Furie."

"His report does mention heroin, but it was not filed until March 2019. All the information contained in my report proves that there's insufficient evidence to continue the incarceration of David Furie and all the drug charges against him be dismissed."

The judge glanced at the DA.

"Do you have any information that you'd like to present to this court that would differ from what we've just heard?"

"No, your honor," he answered.

"Good—so let's sum up the evidence presented in this case. This courtroom did not know during Mr. Furie's trial, but it knows now, that a comprehensive review of the incident has been conducted by the defense. This includes interviews of civilian and law enforcement witnesses as well as a review of physical evidence, Body Camera footage, medical reports, and reports from the Natick Police Department."

He paused for a moment and adjusted the position of his glasses over his nose. Then he looked directly at the DA.

"The person to blame is the lead officer in this case, Officer Karl Toomey. If he had been honest and done his job correctly, we wouldn't be here. Before vacating the charges," he added, "it was clear that he and a sworn witness, Mr. Glenn Ordway, had committed perjury at the trial. Do you agree?"

"Yes, your honor."

"If you're satisfied with everything we've heard here today. I see no reason why I should not sign a motion for Mr. Furie's immediate release and all charges against him be dismissed. Do you agree?"

"Yes, your honor."

Then the judge looked at David and his attorney. "Congratulations, Mr. Furie, you're a free man. Enjoy the day."

Raucous cheers and laughter followed. His attorney shook his hand while a host of friends embraced him and slapped him on the back.

A triumphant smile played around David's lips and his eyes searched for Alesha.

Amid the crush of television cameras and reporters, she and Jenny could hardly be seen.

"See you later!" Alesha cried out, waving her hand to get his attention. "Lunch is on me!"

One reporter managed to break away from his colleagues and filed this report:

After a year behind bars, David Furie, a star football player at Natick North High School, walked out of court a free man today.

Furie, 19, was freed by Framingham Superior Court Judge Stephen Kaplansky, after a reexamination of the case by Furie's attorney uncovered a deeply flawed investigation.

Drugs were allegedly found at Furie's home following an altercation in which 44-year-old Bill Parham was seriously injured. However, no drugs were ever found or mentioned in any police report.

Parham remains in a coma at Boston Memorial Hospital.

Chapter 29

The death of an extremely close relative is a terrible thing for anyone to endure, especially for a person as young as David. He was fortunate, however, to have such a close support team as he did, but he felt there was something missing in his life.

While eating lunch at Wellmans, he seemed to be in awe of his friends scurrying around, maneuvering so nonchalantly, effortlessly while he stumbled around like he was deaf and blind not knowing which way to go, too prideful to ask.

Alesha noticed how slowly he was eating so she slipped her arm between his and snuggled close.

"You've hardly touched your burger. Are you feeling OK?" she asked.

"Yeah—yeah—I'm fine. I just have a lot of things on my mind."

She knew he was still dealing with some problems so she did her best to cheer him up.

"It's so good to have you back in my life. While you were away, all I could think about was that first day we met. Remember?"

"Yeah—I thought about that a lot. It helped to get me through those long days at Danbury."

"Now you should start thinking about going to college and becoming a professional football player."

"She's right," said Jenny. "We're all behind you and we'll never stop supporting you."

"Thanks," he said, taking a big bite out of his burger, and washing it down with a glass of Coke. "With friends like you two—"

"And Chris makes three. He's coming home tonight, so we're having dinner with him."

"Awesome," said David. "It'll be great seeing him again."

Chapter 30
Providence, Rhode Island

Following David's trial, Bill Parham's name was out there for everyone to see. But only one person seemed to be interested.

His name: Richie *the Lizard* Amaral.

His job: Longtime boss of a local crime family, whose control extended throughout New England for more than three decades.

He had the combined talents of toughness, intellect, experience, and would not hesitate to have anyone who stood in his way 'eliminated'.

He snapped his fingers together to draw his bodyguard's attention.

"Hey Wimpy, turn off the TV and get over here. I've got an important job for you."

Wimpy was a little ponderous, but it was his plump 250 pound body which made him so. He was attractive in a slovenly way, with a mass of jet-black curls, dark eyes and olive-colored skin.

"OK boss," he answered, hurrying over to Richie's desk and plopping himself down in a leather armchair.

Richie took a long puff at his cigar and pulled a small black notebook out of his pocket.

"Do you remember that mole, the one who disappeared two years ago with 40 K after Giansolo was killed?"

"Yeah, sort of a smooth talker; liked the ladies; that guy?"

"That's him. Well, the money he was supposed to give to Giansolo belonged to me."

"So whaddya want me to do?"

He ripped a piece of paper out of his notebook, scribbled something on it and handed it to Wimpy.

"That's the address of the hospital that Parham's in. Drive up to Boston and see if there's anyone spending an unusual amount of time hanging around him."

"While I'm there, is there anything else that you want me to do?"

"No, nothing else, understand? There's somebody who knows where he stashed all that loot. I want to know who that person is."

***

No actor could have put on a better performance than Rose Gutierrez the day she went to see Bill Parham.

She was dressed in a gray casual mini dress with roll short sleeves and a chic tie waist front, and white ankle boots.

She didn't have any trouble convincing his doctor that she was Parham's fiancé.

Her features, even and firm, her lips plump and glimmering with sparkly gloss, charmed him.

There was a tinge of sadness in her voice as she showed him a photograph of them together and told him about their romantic days in Puerto Rico.

When he took her in to see him, her hand moved to her mouth as she tried to damp down the panic.

There was hardly any color in his cheeks, nor expression on his face. And the only things keeping him alive were a respirator and feeding tubes.

He was the opposite of the well-dressed, smooth talking man that she once knew. And each day that passed made it less likely that he would come out of the coma.

Over the next few weeks, his doctor noticed that she was the only person who spent a lot of time at his bedside.

The abrupt stop in communication and contact was heartbreaking, her constant thought of him alone in the hospital upsetting.

But that didn't stop her from asking one very important question. *What chance does he have of recovering from a coma?*

His answer was brief and to the point.

"A coma seldom lasts longer than several weeks. People who are unconscious for a longer time might transition to a persistent vegetative state

107

or brain death. Since you're the closest person to him, you've got to make a decision soon whether to keep him on life-support, or pull the plug."

"Isn't there anything else that you could do to help him recover?"

He paused before answering. "There is, but I don't usually administer it to patients who are this far along. It's called a coma cocktail. It's a combined mixture of glucose, naloxone (Narcan) and thiamin."

"If it helps him to recover, go ahead; use it."

"Before I do, may I suggest that you try playing some music for him, something he may remember? I can have a nurse put some earphones on him. Sometimes that helps."

"If you think it will—please do."

Chapter 31

Not until David moved into the Wellman's carriage house did he know that Mr. Wellman once worked for the federal office that tracked down WWII-era Nazis in the United States and moved to revoke their citizenship and deport them.

The only clue he had were several Outstanding Performance Awards from the Office of Special Investigations hanging from the walls of his study.

He read them with much satisfaction, for they disclosed a truly revengeful feeling, a desire to undo as much trouble as those two liars, Toomey and Ordway, had caused.

But first, he'd have to find them. And even if he did, what would his next move be? Perhaps Chris could answer that question.

"Your parents were very hospitable, asking me to move in with you guys. I would have had trouble going back to my house and not finding my parents there," he said.

"I can only imagine how you would've felt," Chris replied, changing the subject. "Do you plan to accept that scholarship to Harvard?"

"I should, but there's something standing in my way."

"Like what?"

He gave a very vivid and often troubling account of his time in prison.

"Danbury really screwed up my mind; lying awake at night in a jail cell, thinking about all that time I could've spent taking care of my mother; bad thoughts constantly popping up in my head. When I finally dozed off, I'd have recurring nightmares about those two liars and how I'd get even with them after I got out."

Chris's gaze lingered before he continued their conversation.

"It's all over; time to move on."

"You and I are like brothers, so I hope you don't mind if I ask you a personal question?"

"No—not at all."

"I saw where your father was awarded several performance awards from the Justice Department's Office of Special Investigations for tracking down Nazis. That's pretty impressive."

"He seldom talks about it, but he when he does, it always centers on his belief that for *those people* to live freely in the United States, is contrary to everything this country stands for."

"Your father's quite a guy."

"Yeah—he was given one of those awards for helping to put in place a sophisticated system that allowed the office's historians to check wartime German personnel records against US immigration records."

"You're proud of him, huh?"

"He had a tough job that many thought was impossible to accomplish, but he proved it could be done."

"I remember asking for your advice once before; it was very helpful. Do you mind if I bug you again?"

Chris was taken aback by David's sudden mood change and shifted in his seat uncomfortably.

"You're full of questions today. You don't plan to do anything stupid, do you?"

"I have no intention of doing *anything stupid*. I was just wondering what I'd do if push comes to shove."

"No pun intended, but don't forget what happened the last time you got into a *pushing* match with somebody."

"I haven't forgotten."

"If you ever come face to face with those two liars, you'd achieve much more by persuasion than brute force."

"If you were in my place, wouldn't you want to know why they told such blatant lies? There's got to be a reason."

Chris scratched his head thoughtfully. "I don't know. But why don't you just wait and see what that internal investigation turns up."

Some doubt lingered in his mind. "I don't think it really matters. Those two guys are still going to be out there on the street messing up people's lives."

"I think it's time for you to focus your thoughts on more worldly matters."

"Like what?"

Chris gave him a brief straightforward answer.

"Like going to college and carving out a future."

David smiled but suddenly his smile faded and that doubtful shadow passed over his face again.

"You're still my quarterback, huh?"

"Only when it comes to steering you in the right direction," he answered with a reassuring pat on David's shoulder. "Now go get dressed so we won't be late for dinner."

***

It was a happy, but quiet, little dinner that evening with Alesha and Jenny.

Halfway through their meal, Alesha noticed there was something in David's demeanor that suggested he was anxious.

As hard as he tried, he couldn't shake that gnawing, revengeful feeling that he had earlier. It had made its way into the dining room and it was lurking around the edges of his conversation.

After supper, she suggested they go for a walk and try to put in order the whirling thoughts that pulsed through him.

"Something is troubling you," she said. "Mind telling me what it is?"

The passion he felt during their first walk through the park, he felt no longer, only an indefinable sadness and tension which he couldn't understand.

"I'm sorry, but I'm still angry about the lies those two assholes told during my trial."

"I thought so," she said, squeezing his hand gently. "I understand why that continues to bother you."

"I'm glad somebody does."

"Even so, my coach once told me that holding on to anger is like grasping a hot coal with the intent of throwing it at someone else, except you're the one who gets burned."

He smiled slightly. "He sounds just like my former coach."

"This Saturday, I'm flying to Australia with my team to compete in an ATP tournament. I'll be gone for about two months. You need a change of scene so why don't you come with me?"

"I'd love too. But I have to take care of some unfinished business."

He took her arm and led her toward the dense group of pine trees that surrounded the lake.

"Remember the first time we were here? How we almost made love?"

She blushed; her dark eyes brightened, appearing almost luminous. "Yes, I do. It was a lovely moonlight night, just like this, quiet and peaceful."

"It was until that lying cop entered our lives."

The smooth surface of the lake reflected back the brilliant moonlight on his face and she noticed an unusual flush in his cheeks.

"David honey, I hope you don't mind me saying this, but you've been acting sort of strange all night. Do you think you should see a shrink?"

"You think I'm crazy, huh?"

"No, but I think you need someone who can help get rid of whatever is troubling you."

"I'll give it a shot while you're gone."

"Promise?" she said.

"I promise," he answered, kissing her on both cheeks before his lips found hers.

Her hair whipped around her face in the wind before she gently released herself from his embrace.

"I'm going to miss you, terribly," she said.

"Me too," he replied. "Bring home a trophy for me."

"I will," she replied, her cheeks tinted with the crisp air; her eyes dancing with the brisk walk home through the park.

Chapter 32

David continued to have trouble sleeping that night. Tormented by his conscience, he continually squeezed his eyes shut, and laid still, tiny beads of sweat streaming from his brow. It was nearly 5 AM before he finally decided to slip on a sweat suit and go jogging.

Upon his return, he was surprised to see Mr. Wellman sitting on the back porch, reading the morning newspaper.

"You're up early," he said. "Trouble sleeping?"

"Yes, so I thought I'd go for a short run. I'm sorry if I woke you."

"Don't worry about it," he said, glancing at his watch with the same measured composure that he did with everything.

"My kitchen staff usually arrives around this time. I'll give you a key so you can come and go as you please."

"Thank you, sir. I hope you don't mind me saying this, but I was really impressed by those performance awards hanging in your study."

He shrugged his shoulders as though it was no big thing.

"A lot of credit has to go to the FBI and the US Army who helped us track down Nazis."

"How difficult was that?"

"I owe that to my father. He repeatedly impressed on me the value of hard work. So it wasn't difficult patching together information that reached me at a classroom level in a fragmented and sometimes confusing way."

"What if I told you that I want to track down—"

Mr. Wellman cut him off.

"I already talked to Chris. He told me that you still want to get even with those two liars."

"Ever since getting out of prison, I've been trying to shake off the bitter feelings that creep inside my head. No matter how hard I try, they're still there."

"I wouldn't consider that culture shock. It's more of a mental problem; like feeling guilty because you left behind some unfinished business before and after your mother died."

"So, how do I get rid of it?"

"I'm not a psychologist, but *I am* your godfather. So I don't want you to get involved in anything that I've been doing for twenty years."

"Pardon me," David said, his attention now totally concentrated.

"I wouldn't expect you to know this, but Bill Parham and Karl Toomey are members of the American Nazi Party. And Ordway belongs to the racist group, The Proud Men."

"How did you find that out?" David asked, surprised that Mr. Wellman knew something about their affiliation with hate groups.

"Neither one of them had a red flag attached to their body. But after you were sent to Danbury, your attorney and I did a little investigating of our own. We were able to open up a whole new barrel of rotting fish."

David remained wrapped in thought, his mind somewhat confused by the sudden influx of information.

"This might come as sort of a surprise," Mr. Wellman continued, "but during your trial, all Toomey and Ordway had to do is convince the jury that you had done something wrong, something that would land you in jail."

"There's got to be a reason why they did that?"

"They're either covering up for someone or there's something going on that we don't know anything about."

"I don't get it."

"Let me put it another way," Mr. Wellman responded.

"Propaganda rests on what people already believe, and the negative things they hear over and over again. Take Hitler's book *Mein Kampf,* for example. It contains rumors which eventually led to the Holocaust."

"That's powerful stuff; huh?"

"Almost as powerful is another one of his hate filled books; the *Protocols of the Elders of Zion.* It became a part of the propaganda' effort to justify persecution and annihilation of the Jews."

"I've never heard of that book."

"That doesn't surprise me. It's not the kind of book that you'd expect to see in a library."

"You seem to know a lot about those books. I assume you've read them."

"When I went to school in Israel, I was taught about what they contained. They're considered to be the most notorious and widely distributed anti-Semitic publications of modern times."

"It sounds like Hitler was able to sell a whole lot of bullshit to some very weak-minded people."

"I wouldn't exactly call them weak-minded because there are many racists who are not only well educated but come from affluent families."

He glanced at his watch, tucked the newspaper beneath his armpit and stood up.

"I've really enjoyed our conversation, but I've got to go and round up the kitchen staff."

"When you're not so busy, would you mind teaching me Krav Maga?"

Mr. Wellman knew there was a reason behind David's request so he simply answered, "Let's talk about it when there's nobody around."

Chapter 33

Rose Gutierrez was sitting in a chair next to Bill Parham's bed, her elbows on her knees, clasping her head with both hands. She was tired, but she didn't consider the hours she had already spent there, wasted time.

She never considered herself to be a good actor, moreover, a singer with a pleasant voice and a vivacious way of delivering it, especially if they were Spanish songs.

Time was running out for Bill Parham, and she was getting impatient.

He showed no signs of recovery, and since nobody was around, she gently removed his earphones and listened to the song that was playing.

"Qué diablos! (What the hell)," she said aloud, shaking her hands in the air and letting out a groan of frustration.

"No wonder he won't wake up," she added, tossing the earphones aside, "Esos epesta (this sucks)!"

She put her mouth close to his ear and quietly began singing the immensely romantic Spanish song, Bésame, Mucho (Kiss me a lot).

Amazingly, a few minutes later, his eyelids flickered and he slowly opened his eyes.

That song apparently renewed his energy and pulled him out of the coma. Somewhere deep in his mind, he remembered hearing it somewhere.

It also had meaning, as it was the first single he ever bought that reminded him of Rose.

A rush of excitement filled her heart just as a nurse quickly entered his room.

"You weren't supposed to remove these earphones!" she said.

"Why shouldn't I?" Rose fired back. "The music that you were playing for him was horrible. And if you look closely, you'll see that he has opened his eyes."

The nurse gave Rose an irritated glance before turning her attention back to Bill Parham.

Without saying another word, she left the room and soon returned with his doctor.

"This is a good sign, Miss Gutierrez," the doctor said. "But the next time you visit, please consult with me first before taking matters into your own hands."

"I'm sorry. I just didn't want to lose him and I guess I got a little impatient."

"OK, so now you'll have to leave the room while we check his vital signs."

The next few minutes dragged by like hours while she waited, in hushed suspense, not knowing what to expect.

The doctor had made up his mind very clearly what he'd say to Rose; but as he approached her, it was not so easy to say what he was thinking.

He gave a sad, distant half-smile as he looked down at her, and what he said caused her heart to squeeze in her chest.

"Due to his injury and the time he spent in the coma, his body will be greatly affected. And because he's suffering from quadriparesis a weakness in his limbs, he'll have to use a wheelchair until we can get him back on his feet."

"Will he ever walk again?"

"It's possible. Nerve cells," he explained, "can regenerate, but do so only in specific parts of the brain. Plus, it's a very slow process if it does occur."

She had hoped and prayed for a better prognosis and asked calmly, "So I guess he'll have to stay here a little while longer, huh?"

"I recommend that he be sent to our rehab center because minimally conscious people are largely unaware of what's going on around them. They have enough brain activity, though, to have some glimmer of preserved awareness of themselves or the surrounding environment."

She approached his bed, brushed his hair back and kissed him on the forehead.

Her face looked familiar; however, he thought she was someone he'd like to ask out on a date.

"Hi, beautiful—how would you like to go dancing tonight?" he asked, his voice husky and bewildered as he gazed up at her.

She touched his lips, not knowing whether he was awake enough to know he had spoken aloud.

"I'd love to mi cariño," she answered. "As soon as you can walk again, we'll go dancing every night."

Chapter 34

The desire for revenge can be overpowering. It bred a feeling of helplessness within David—that he was powerless to oppose the so-called *liars* whose testimonies sent him to jail.

Mr. Wellman knew, from his own past experiences while growing up in Czechoslovakia, that David's recovery was as much mental and psychological as anything else.

Bewildered by the whirl of horrible thoughts that followed after seeing several of his neighbors executed by the Schutzstaffel (SS), he often found himself wishing he could protect those around him who were intimidated, or punished for no reason at all.

As an adult, the most effective way he could do that would be to continue to help track down WWII-era Nazis in the United States.

But, it wasn't an easy job. WWII-era Nazis were spread out all across the US, from Sacramento to Syracuse, courtesy of the German American Bund and its elected leader, Fritz Shtoler.

Shtoler was initially effective as a leader and was able to unite the organization and expand its membership.

Mr. Hellman had learned quite a bit about him while he was working for the US Government. And Shtoler soon became his nemesis.

There wasn't much he could do to stop him from uniting the Bund and dividing the US into three so-called Gaue: Gau Ost (East), Gau West and Gau Midwest.

Shtoler followed that up by establishing a number of neo-Nazi training camps, several of them in New York and New Jersey.

Their population grew fast, and eventually they had recruited enough people to hold rallies displaying the Nazi insignia and using the Hitler salute to greet each other. They attacked anything that did not conform to their beliefs.

They even went so far as to show their loyalty to America by displaying the flag of the United States alongside the flag of Nazi Germany at Bund meetings and declared that George Washington was 'the first Fascist' who did not believe democracy would work.

After a year of trailing Shtoler around the country, and watching Nazism bloom like a spring flower, Mr. Hellman came up with a plan that might stop it in its track.

He modified the **Colossus Mark 1** computer system developed in England during World War II, and used to break encrypted German messages. It was the world's first programmable digital computer. And it helped him to keep a watchful eye on Shtoler and his connections across the country.

No one, in any law enforcement agency, ever figured out who it was who triggered a New York tax investigation that determined Shtoler .had embezzled $14,000 from the Bund.

The Bund did not seek to have him prosecuted, operating on the principle that the leader had absolute power. However, New York City's district attorney prosecuted him in an attempt to cripple the Bund. Shtoler was sentenced to two and a half to five years in prison for tax evasion and embezzlement.

While Shtoler was incarcerated, Mr. Hellman saw that his citizenship was revoked. Upon his release after 43 months in state prison, he was re-arrested, as an enemy alien by the federal government and imprisoned at Rikers Island in New York.

A year later, he was deported to Germany.

Mr. Hellman's efforts had paid off.

***

Because David experienced similar mental and psychological problems as Mr. Wellman, he thought they might be related to the unexpected deaths of both his parents.

Eventually, he came to the conclusion that David might be suffering from Post Traumatic Stress Disorder (PTSD) and training him might help to cure his depression and anxiety.

Fear triggers many split-second changes in the body to help defend against danger or to avoid it. He thought.

This 'fight-or-flight' response is a typical reaction meant to protect a person from harm.

At the beginning of his training, David was eager to learn a bunch of kicks and punches so he could be prepared for a fight. He quickly learned that Krav Maga is effective but not in the ways he expected it to be.

"Take time to deliberate; but when the time for action arrives," said Mr. Wellman, "stop thinking and strike first and strike fast."

He was surprised to find that he had the wrong idea about the goals of self-defense. As Mr. Wellman explained; "If you get into a fight, Krav Maga, is always a last resort. Because one blow can shatter a kneecap, crack a skull, or break an arm."

Ahead of David lay several months of intense training. During that time, he added more muscle to his body.

There were many differences between his idea of martial arts and what Krav Maga turned out to be.

"Being the better fighter," Mr. Wellman explained, "isn't all about who has the best moves. It's more about using natural movements and reactions for defense, combined with an immediate and decisive counterattack."

Several times, he allowed David to attack him. Less than a second later, he found himself lying face down on a training mat, his arm twisted behind his back or his neck. It almost didn't register, so smooth and fast, inhumanly fast.

"That," Mr. Wellman explained, "was an example of simultaneous defense and attack while never using both hands in the same defensive movement."

David stood up, pushed back his hair from his forehead and used a towel to swab the sweat off of his face.

"Thank you, sir. I guess you just showed me that the smarter fighter is the one who wins."

"Exactly, and you should never forget that."

Along with his training came a heavy dose of history, both past and present.

He soon learned that history and politics are a tangle of lies and intrigue.

"A lot of what I'm telling you happened a long time ago," Mr. Wellman said, "But Parham and Toomey belong to an organization once known as the German American Bund or German American Federation. Only American citizens of German descent were allowed to join. Today they're known as

Friends of the New Germany. They'll recruit anyone who can wave a German flag or spread propaganda."

"It sounds like their goal, which seems closer to realization now than it was quite a few years ago, hasn't changed."

"They chose their new name after the press criticized them for being unpatriotic."

"Are they?"

"They're openly pro-Nazi, and they've engaged in activities such as storming the German language New Yorker demanding that Nazi-sympathetic articles be published in every copy of their newspaper."

"What about Ordway, know anything about him?"

"Only that he's a 45-year-old resident of Georgia, who occupies Proud Men leadership positions as both the Sergeant of Arms and the President of the Atlanta Chapter. He visited a number of states over the past five years to take part in neo-Nazi demonstrations."

"So, when those two groups get together, they're very good at stirring up trouble."

"Just like tossing gasoline on a fire. They say they love this country and perhaps they do, but they hate what it stands for."

David's manner turned quiet but serious.

"We were taught in school that freedom of expression is a basic human right."

"It is, but when the seed of freedom blooms, it's not supposed to nurture violence," Mr. Wellman replied philosophically.

"Thanks for your advice, encouragement and martial arts training."

"You're welcome."

Mr. Wellman wasn't quite that confident in David's ability. He knew that it took years for a person to become proficient in everything that pertained to law enforcement.

And since David wasn't really a law enforcement officer, he had some doubts as to whether he'd take anything more seriously than his desire to track down the people responsible for sending him to jail.

"I hope you don't mind if I ask you a question."

"No, not at all."

"How do you plan to use everything that I've taught you?"

"Over the past few months, I've come to understand what's been going on inside my head. I'll use it to stay out of trouble."

"I was hoping you'd say that. However, there's one other thing."

"What's that?"

Mr. Wellman's answer was not quite what David expected to hear.

"You may disagree with what I'm about to say, but that guy—Bill Parham did bring a few smiles to your mother's face. And no matter what you think about him, you should show some compassion by dropping by the hospital to see how he's doing."

"Are you suggesting that I forgive him for what he did?"

"Forgiveness doesn't mean condoning or excusing. Forgiveness can mean accepting that we may have done something we regret, but finding a new attitude and perspective toward ourselves in relation to that action. You may never forget what happened that night at your house, but it'll help you find a way to move forward."

A sudden picture of Bill Parham's head crashing into the end table flashed through his mind.

"Yeah, I guess you're right," he replied.

Jacob Rehabilitation Center, 5 PM that evening

Wimpy arrived at sunset, dreary from a tiresome drive; but the dreariness only lasted until he located Bill Parham's room.

"For the next week or so," said the receptionist, "only one person at a time is allowed to visit him and it looks like his fiancé beat you to it."

"His fiancé?" he repeated. "Sorry, if I seem a bit surprised. Even though I'm one of his closest friends, I didn't know he was engaged."

"Yes, and I might add—she's quite the lovely lady. She's been by his side from the very first day he was admitted."

He pointed at a row of chairs sitting on the other side of the lobby.

"Would you mind if I sat over there? When she's through visiting him, I'd like to talk to her about his condition."

"No, not at all. I'll tell her you're here," she answered with a hospitable smile. "She'll be glad to know he has such a caring friend."

Immediately, her attention shifted to the sound of the elevator door as it opened.

"You're in luck," the receptionist said, "she just stepped off the elevator."

Even Wimpy, who never considered himself much of a lady's man, was taken aback by her beauty.

Rose headed directly for the exit door, but he caught up with her and introduced himself.

Her eyes flashed as she felt his fingers upon her arm.

"Sorry miss, if I startled you. My name's Willie, but my friends call me Wimpy. I'm a close friend of Bill's. I dropped by to see him but the receptionist told me that you beat me to it."

At first, she was a little suspicious about how he just popped up out of nowhere.

During Bill's stay in Puerto Rico, he never mentioned anything about having a close friend.

Wimpy's friendly smile, however, left a good impression on her.

"Mine's Rose," she replied. "So, how did you and Bill meet each other?"

"That'd be a good story to tell ovah a drink, and dinnah if you don't have any othah plans."

Her interest in knowing more about Bill from a close friend was obvious, so she merely smiled.

"Pardon me if I seem a bit reluctant. But some people don't know the difference between being friendly and indicating personal interest."

"I've nevah hit on anyone's fiancé and I don't intend to do it now. So whaddya say we grab a cocktail and a bite to eat?"

"It's been awhile since somebody invited me out for dinner so I guess that'd be OK. Do you have any place in mind?"

"Wait here a second. I'll ask the receptionist if she knows of a nice comfortable spot nearby."

Chapter 35

Sunlight shined on David as he steered his gray Chevy into the Sumner Tunnel. Natick was farther away now and his destination closer. The radio purred from rock and roll music pulsating as he turned on to the Mystic River Bridge.

Halfway across, the view of the Boston skyline was stunning.

Some doubt still subsisted in his mind whether he was doing the right thing.

Several times during his drive, he thought about turning around and heading back home.

But he had made a promise to Mr. Wellman, a promise he meant to keep.

Thirty minutes later, he walked into the lobby of the Rehabilitation Center.

The receptionist looked up at him and asked, "Can I help you?"

"I'm here to see Bill Parham," he replied.

"My, my, he certainly is popular tonight," she said, uniformly polite, chatty and cheerful with visitors. "First his fiancé dropped by, then a friend, and now you."

"His fiancé and a friend?"

"Yes—but he didn't seem to be as interested in seeing Mr. Parham as he did in taking her out for dinner."

"I see," David said, his head swirling with several afterthoughts? *Who are his fiancé and his friend? And was he engaged while he was seeing my mother?*

"He's in room 440," she said, handing him a visitor's pass.

"Thanks, but I won't need that right now. With all this excitement going on around him, perhaps he should get some rest."

"That's very considerate of you."

"How long ago did they leave?"

She glanced at her watch. "Oh, I'd say about five minutes ago. If you plan to join them for dinner, you'll find them at *Coco's Cajun Seafood* restaurant right across the street."

"Just so I'll recognize them, what were they wearing?"

"She had on a bright red dress with an open back. With her movie star looks, she'll be hard to miss. And he was sort of a pudgy guy wearing khaki pants and a blue sports coat."

He smiled kindly at her. "Thank you so much."

I'm quite sure they'll share quite a bit of information on how they met *Bill Parham*, thought David.

Upon entering the restaurant, he asked to be seated near them.

He eavesdropped on everything they said; how she met Bill Parham in Puerto Rico, and how he became his business partner.

Two martinis and a bottle of wine later, her lips loosened even more.

She hadn't socialized in quite a while so she relaxed and told him everything he wanted to hear; where she lived, and why she left her husband for another man.

She even talked about the so-called 'friendship' key, hanging around her neck.

In exchange, he lied to her about how he planned to visit the hospital so he could learn more about Bill's condition.

When dinner was over, he offered her a ride home, which she gratefully accepted.

A few seconds later, David left the restaurant, jumped in his car, and followed them to a three-decker in Waltham.

He pulled over to the curb and watched as she staggered out of Wimpy's car on trembling legs, gave him a return wave and entered the house.

***

Her first-floor apartment, perfectly designed for a single person, was on a very quiet street.

She had lived there for a while and when she wasn't visiting Bill Parham, she thoroughly enjoyed the solitude.

Aside from a small kitchen, TV, her bed, wardrobe, and a couch, there was little need for more.

She undressed, snapped off the lights and climbed into bed.

Ten minutes later, she was fast asleep.

Wimpy sat in his car for a half hour, talking on his cell phone to his boss, Richie *the Lizard* Amaral.

He gave Wimpy explicit instructions to kidnap her and bring her to Providence.

He slipped on a pair of black gloves, reached into his glove compartment and pulled out a small black tool kit.

He climbed out of his car and tiptoed around to the back of Rose's apartment.

Using a glass cutter, he made a shallow score along the surface of a pane of glass that would break into two pieces, big enough for him to reach the window lock.

He climbed over the windowsill, entered a narrow, dark hall and listened intently for a few minutes. Then he removed a small bottle of chloroform and a handkerchief from his pocket.

He took several steps toward her bed.

Blinded, he tripped over a stool and ducked into a corner, chest heaving, his body slick with sweat.

He peeked around the corner and saw that the sound had not roused her from a deep sleep.

Still, he had to be careful. So he listened.

All he could hear was a sharp intake of her breath in front of him.

He tiptoed over to her bed and noticed that she lay on her back, her head tipped to the side, resting on her shoulder.

He poured a small amount of chloroform on his handkerchief and pressed it gently over her mouth.

Struggling with consciousness, she immediately noticed the intense burning in her throat.

His warm hand on her neck caused her to instinctively turn her head away, knocking the handkerchief on to the floor.

Awake now, she screamed, "Get out!" kicking her feet and swinging at him with her fists.

"I'll brain you if you don't keep quiet," he growled, his voice quiet and menacing.

"Get the fuck away from me!" she shouted, earning a punch to her cheek from his balled up fist. The blow stunned her.

He slung her over his shoulder in one smooth movement.

Fortunately for Rose, David used the same window to gain entrance to her apartment.

"Put her down," he ordered, causing Wimpy to quickly turn around and stare at him.

"Who the fuck are you?" he asked, surprised to find David standing a few feet away from him, his hands hanging loosely by his side.

"It doesn't matter who I am. Just put her down."

"She's coming with me. So get the fuck out of my way," he warned, dumping Rose back on the bed and reaching for his gun.

The barrel of the gun was less than a foot away when David decided to act.

He ducked to the opposite side of Wimpy, swatted his arm away, twisted his waist and kicked him behind the knee.

Moving farther in the same direction, he bounced an elbow off of his jaw.

Wimpy was unconscious before he hit the floor.

"Hey!" shouted the landlord peering over the second floor railing, "What the hell is going on down there!"

Stuck between awareness and blackness, Rose tried to stand; a mistake that left her woozy and disorientated.

"What happened?" she asked, rubbing her sore jaw.

"That guy was trying to kidnap you," he answered, picking up Wimpy's gun and tucking it beneath his belt. "We've got to get out of here just in case more of his goons show up."

"How do I know you're not one of them," she asked, slipping on a bathrobe and quickly stuffing her clothes into a suitcase.

"You've got to trust me because right now I don't have a lot of time to explain," the sound of sirens a few blocks away.

Chapter 36

While driving home, David was quiet long enough to rouse her interest, and she was eager to determine the cause of his silence. "Now, would you mind telling me what the hell is going on?"

"I should be asking you that question."

"I have no idea what you're talking about."

"Does the name David Furie ring a bell?"

For a moment, she gazed up at him with a wary expression on her face and in her eyes. Several seconds later, her nervous look was replaced by calm acceptance.

"Dios mio (my god)," she sputtered, "I knew you looked familiar. You're—"

"Yeah, yeah," he said, interrupting her, "I'm the guy who put Bill Parham in the hospital."

"So, how come you showed up right after that tirón (jerk) tried to kidnap me?"

"I think you have something that somebody wants. And since you're Bill Parham's fiancé, perhaps you're the only person who knows what it is."

She was quiet for a while and thought about what he had just said.

"Aha!" she said, snapping her fingers. "He took some pictures of me a while ago, and he said he was going to show them to an agent. He also gave me one of his business cards."

"Do you remember anything else?"

"He didn't exactly give it to me but I found this key when I packed up his clothes. I thought it would be nice to wear it as a memento."

He stared at her for a moment and noticed the key hanging from a silver chain around her neck. "That's got to be it."

"What do you mean?"

"I don't think those pictures and that card are as important as the key. After we get to my place, would you mind if I borrowed it?"

"No, not at all, as long as you don't mind me asking where your place is."

"Natick. You'll be safe there. By the way, what's your name?"

"Rose Gutierrez."

David didn't know the kidnapper's identity and from this moment on he realized that he couldn't trust anyone.

"I'm sorry that we had to meet this way, but I'm trying to figure out a few things."

"Is that why you showed up tonight at my house?" she asked, wiping her tired eyes, an ache fluttering through her chin at the lingering scent of chloroform.

"It's a good thing that I did."

"I'm sorry but that doesn't answer my question."

"There's some sort of a connection between the kidnapper and Bill Parham. And why I spent time in prison because of it?"

For a moment, she looked confused. "Todavía no entiendo (I still don't understand)."

"If you still have that card, turn on the overhead light and tell me what it says."

She fumbled around in her pocketbook before she pulled out the card.

"One side has his address and telephone number. And on the other side, someone scribbled the name, Glenn Ordway, his address, and the letters ANP. Below that there's some letters and numbers."

"I might have to borrow that, too."

Her voice turned to a whisper, and he could tell she was either crying or close to it.

"You can, just as long as you promise not to do anything that's going to cause me or Bill any trouble."

He looked at her, conflicted. "You love him, huh?"

"Let's just say that I care a lot about him."

After arriving at his apartment, he turned his car around and parked so it faced the drive, ready to leave at a moment's notice.

"You'll be safe here," he said, pointing at a dimly lit window over the garage door. "I'm going to let you in so you can unpack and get comfortable."

Once safely inside, he felt an urge to offer some modicum of comfort to this woman he hardly knew. He also hoped that sleep would remove some of the confusion from her night.

"The bed is yours; I'll sleep on the couch."

Two wing-backed chairs and a comfortable sofa sank into a Persian rug, but what caught her full attention was a queen-sized waterbed.

The shower was fitted with warm air heating to create a perfect drying space.

"There are clean facecloths and towels in the bathroom. Run some cold water on one of them and press it against your jaw. It'll help reduce some of the swelling."

"I really appreciate your hospitality," she replied, unlatching the chain from around her neck and handing him the key.

"Thanks," he said, tucking it into his pocket. "I've got to run an errand. I should be back shortly. While I'm gone, relax and take care of that jaw."

After he left, she was tortured by the thought she might have waited too long to realize the value of the key. So she took a shower.

Afterwards, she paced his apartment until she was too tired to stand.

***

On his way to the Framingham Bus Terminal, David kept sorting through the facts as he knew them.

Why wasn't she curious about what Bill Parham stored in the locker? Why was that thug trying to kidnap her?

And what reason did he have for carrying a card with Toomey's name on it, a swastika and a jumble of strange letters and numbers scribbled on the back?

Frustrated, he banged the palm of his hand down on the steering wheel, unable to believe that he was once again involved in something bizarre and treacherous. Or perhaps they had been there from the moment he entered Danbury Prison, right up until now.

Suddenly, he calmed down. The days he spent training with Mr. Wellman taught him many important things. One in particular was a quote from Sun Tzu's acclaimed book, *The Art of War*:

"When it has rained upstream, the stream's flow intensifies. Stop fording. Wait for it to calm."

He realized that somewhere there were answers to all of these lingering questions. He had no other choice than to deal with them one at a time.

Inside the terminal, David spotted several rows of lockers. One of them matched the number on the key. Fortunately, Bill had kept his rental charges up to date, making the locker easy to open.

He inserted the key and the door of the locker opened outward. He reached inside, retrieved a brown paper bag and quickly exited.

It was nearly 6 AM before he returned to his apartment.

He snatched Mr. Wellman's crumpled up newspaper off of the front porch and dashed upstairs, only to find Rose asleep on the couch.

The sound of his shoes on the floor caused her to awake with a start. "Good morning," she said, rubbing her swollen jaw. "What time is it?"

"A little after six," he answered, emptying the contents of the bag on to the table.

Rose's brows furrowed, and she sat straight up. "Where'd you get all that money?"

"Remember the key that you loaned me? Well, it fit into a locker that Bill Parham rented at the Framingham Bus Terminal."

"Dios mio (*my god*)," she said, thumbing through a stack of one-hundred-dollar bills. "There's got to be more than ten thousand dollars here."

"Why don't you count it while I fix us some breakfast?"

Suddenly his doorbell rang, interrupting their conversation.

The sound startled her.

"Who's that?" she asked fearfully, thinking the kidnapper had tracked her down.

"Shhh," David whispered, pressing his index fingers to his lips and reaching for Wimpy's gun.

She quickly stuffed the money back into the bag and hurried out of the kitchen.

He pressed the buzzer and asked, "Who is it?"

Mr. Wellman's voice crackled over the intercom. "Either you got lost on the way to the hospital. Or you forgot to put your clothes on before you went jogging."

"Just a moment, sir," David answered.

He took the phone away from his mouth and signaled for Rose to stay out of sight until he had a chance to explain her presence.

"I fixed you some breakfast. And it's not going to stay hot very long, so buzz me in," urged Mr. Wellman.

Upon entering the apartment, he asked a legitimate question that deserved a thoughtful answer.

"Why don't you save us both sometime and tell me where you've been all night?"

"I didn't have any problem getting to the hospital, but instead of seeing Mr. Parham, I bumped into his—ah—his fiancé."

Mr. Wellman set the tray of food down on the table and gave him an unbelieving stare.

"Really and what happened after that?"

"Someone tried to kidnap her."

"I suppose the next thing you're going to tell me is that this all happened in Waltham, and that you rescued her."

"That's exactly what happened."

Mr. Wellman picked up the newspaper and turned to the third page.

"Call it a coincidence, but I think you both made the news. Here, read this."

A 40-year-old man has been arrested and charged following the attempted kidnapping of a woman in Waltham.

The man, identified by police as William 'Wimpy' Owens, has also been charged with reckless endangerment and acting in a manner injurious to the tenants living in the house.

Surveillance footage released by police shows Owens getting out of a maroon-colored sedan and moving quickly toward the house where the intended victim, identified as 35-year-old Rose Guitterez, lived.

She was last seen leaving the house located at 120 Lakeview Terrace with another unidentified man.

Police continue their search for the couple.

He dropped the paper on the table and poured himself a cup of coffee. "Honestly, I didn't think my evening would end that way."

"How long do you think you can keep her here before the police find out where she is?"

"If it's OK by you, as long as I have to. I thought it might be a good idea if she didn't tip anyone off by filing a police report."

"So you think she's connected in some way to your case?"

"Maybe she is, I don't know."

Mr. Wellman's gaze shifted to the bedroom door as Rose's curly black head peeked around the corner and her dark eyes locked onto his.

"I apologize for interrupting your conversation, but perhaps I can answer that question," she said.

He smiled warmly and stared at her, obviously confused.

"So, you're the mystery woman, huh? Well, maybe you can tell us why somebody would want to kidnap you."

"I don't know. But this whole story is beginning to sound like something out of a movie," she replied, a mystery lurking behind every look exchanged between them.

"The answer might be right here," she said, emptying the contents of the paper bag out on the table.

"She also gave me one of Parham's business cards with Ordway's name and some scribbles on the back," added David.

"Now we're getting somewhere," said Mr. Wellman, who eyed the card thoughtfully and finally nodded.

"That card may have answered both of those questions. Let's not forget that Parham was a very gifted con man who made a living off of unsuspecting individuals."

"Like my mother?" David intoned.

"Unfortunately, she was just one of his victims. He had no one to care about. And that's what made him free enough to be what he was. It's possible that none of that money actually belonged to him."

Rose nibbled on a piece of toast and listened to their conversation with breathless interest. She thought back to the way Bill Parham conned her husband into believing he was running a legitimate gambling operation.

"As for Ordway," Mr. Wellman continued, "I've known for quite some time that he's a member of the Proud Boys. Most likely, he jotted down his address and telephone number to get Parham to join."

"What about those letters and numbers?"

"I believe that's some sort of code that Ordway used to communicate with his friends."

David sat back in his chair, a thought stirring in his mind.

"It wouldn't surprise me if that cop was part of this scheme."

"I wouldn't jump to any conclusion until we know more about him, but that card tells us a hell of a lot about Ordway."

"You've advised me before to stay out of trouble. But I keep getting this strong urge to find the person who paid him to testify against me."

"There's a lot of intrigue attached to your story that's probably why you feel the way you do."

He put his hand on David's shoulder and looked directly into his eyes.

"I have a feeling that you intend to go after Ordway and I'm not going to stop you. However, promise me that you'll be careful so you don't end up in jail again."

"I'm sorry that I got you caught up in this mess, but it looks like we're in it up to our necks."

"You don't have to apologize. This is not the first time that I've been involved in a rather intriguing mystery. In fact, I sort of like it," he said with a wide smile. "Just remember what I taught you. Don't let your emotions interfere with what you intend to do."

"Do you mind if Rose stays here until I get back?"

"Don't worry; my wife and I will keep a close eye on her. Now eat something and get some rest before you leave."

"Thank you, sir."

"You're going to travel to places that you've never been before and you might face a minimum amount of danger. So you've got to be extremely careful."

During his days with the US Special Investigations Unit of the Justice Department, Mr. Wellman used a series of disguises, many of which gained him a reputation for trickery.

Some of his disguises included hats, wigs, glasses, and sticks on facial hair.

He suggested that David do the same.

Chapter 37

David wasn't involved in anything illegal, so he had no reason to be concerned about using some of Bill Parham's money, ten thousand of which he felt belonged to his mother.

He rented a room at the Candler Hotel, an elegant five-star hotel located at the southern tip of downtown Atlanta.

Surrounded by magnificent magnolias and opulent oaks, it overlooked Interstate 85.

He didn't waste any time finding Ordway. He lived a few miles down the road in Glenwood Park, a newly developed area filled with independently owned restaurants, coffee shops, and stores.

It was 6 AM before Ordway left his house.

Using a pair of high-powered binoculars, David watched him climb into a pickup truck and drive over to the Busy Bee Café, where a line of customers waited outside to be seated.

Several minutes elapsed before David was seated on a stool at the bar, not far away.

He ordered scrambled eggs, grits, a side of spam and a glass of orange juice.

Ordway was soon joined by a man wearing a t-shirt, the confederate flag tattooed on his right arm; on his left, a bald eagle with crossed automatic rifles beneath it.

The hate in his bloodshot eyes and bloated face was frightening.

Something else caught David's eye; the butt of a Smith & Wesson double-action revolver in a holster hanging from his belt.

Breakfast finished, Ordway and his friend hopped into their pickups and headed toward the Interstate.

He followed them to the first roundabout before they turned left, through the woods and down a bumpy road. It gradually narrowed and climbed through hills choked with brush and huge oak trees.

He pulled his car off the road into a grassy parking lot and shut off the engine.

In front of him sat an old Civil War era mansion that had an atmosphere of genteel elegance and decay. Inside, the air was stale, reeking of cigar and cigarette smoke.

Beyond the main room were two hallways and a large ballroom overflowing with people.

Some of the attendees wore matching white tees, sunglass and bandannas over their faces, all while holding a massive sign that read *Defend American Labor—CLOSE THE BORDER*.

David sat down in a dimly lit corner and watched as the guest speaker entered.

Seeing him, the audience reacted as if they had been struck by a lightning bolt.

Heads turned, everyone's eyes focused on him, a deafening applause followed.

Hate appeared to be speaking from every line of his face.

Tattooed on his arm was a Celtic cross surrounded by a circle, one of the most commonly used white supremacist symbols, and an SS (*Schutzstaff*) that represented the Nazi Paramilitary Organization.

"The laws of this country are antiquated and have no contemporary relevance," he bellowed. "America is no longer what our forefathahs intended it to be. Instead, it has become a land of antiquated social rules and liberal suffocating traditions. Y'all know that Jews, Blacks, Spicks and Antifa are responsible for the troubles that exist in this country."

A loud applause followed.

"If we don't take it upon ourselves to change things now, everything that our forefathahs did to build a country around our beliefs, our traditions, and our love for each othah are doomed to failure."

Everyone stood up, clapped, and cheered loudly.

Others seemed to regard the American flag as the harbinger of a new era and waved it briskly in the air.

Following his speech, a series of short instructional presentations on the tactics and strategy of guerrilla warfare were presented.

Several men dressed in bullet-proof vests and helmets led the gathering to a neighboring meadow where they practiced their marksmanship.

David stood and watched as they fired their weapons at targets that normally displayed bull's eyes. Replacing them were dark faces with question marks in the center.

"Now think of those bull's eyes as someone who you'd considah to be an enemy," the instructor said. "Focus on controlling your breathing and keep your eyes on the target!"

David blocked his ears as a cacophony of loud gunshots echoed across the open field.

These folks really mean business, he thought to himself.

Several minutes elapsed before he felt someone standing right behind him, way too close for comfort.

Whoever it was shouted into his ear. "You look a little bit gun-shy so why don't you just stand over there and watch."

David turned around to find Ordway and his friend, who tugged at a leash around the neck of a German Police dog, staring at him.

Even though he arrived on the scene in disguise, he drew a few shaky breaths to calm himself. "Don't mind if I do," he replied.

He quickly realized that his presence had just turned into his worst nightmare.

Will my chances of escape be diminished by taking the time to watch target practice?

Ordway's friend turned his head and spit out some tobacco-loaded saliva that landed near David's shoe.

"We haven't seen you around, heyah before. Mind if I ask where you're from?"

David had to think fast. "No, not at all. I'm from Boston."

"We plan to hold a Unite the Right Rally there sometime next month to double our recruiting efforts," said Ordway.

His friend added a toothy remark. "Last time we were theyah we tried to sneak intah the back of the St. Patrick's Day parade but the police stopped us. They claimed we nevah registered with the city and they treated us like protestahs. We're not gonna make that same mistake again. We're gonna make them respect us."

Ordway's tone was gruff, his gaze intent. It was if he was trying to figure out if he recognized David beneath his false beard and dyed blond hair.

"Maybe you'd like to join us—ah—Mr—"

"Oops, I forgot to introduce myself. It's Bennie, Bennie Franklin."

"I'm pleased to meet you. My friends just call me T-man," said Ordway. "The weapons we use here are under close supervision. The pistol is my favorite, but the rifle has more power. So whaddya say—care to join us?"

"I'd like to," said David, glancing at his wristwatch. "But I promised my girlfriend that I'd take her to lunch."

"I hope you don't mind if I ask you if we've met someplace before?"

"I don't think so."

"So, how'd you find us?"

"A close friend of mine told me about how you folks are expanding your recruiting efforts. And since I'm just another guy who wants to make things better for this country, I thought I'd check you out."

To say that he wasn't scared would be an understatement. He wanted to run out of there like there was a bear on his butt.

However, his past experience with Brutus taught him something. If you're nervous, a dog will pick up on those feelings and become more anxious himself.

Ordway started to say something but David quickly waved his hand and smiled. "I'm sorry, but I have to leave. You know how women are when you're late for a date."

"No problem. We'll be here for a couple of more days."

"Thanks for the invite. I'll keep that in mind."

Ordway nodded, but didn't offer to shake David's hand. "Good, see you around."

Without saying another word, David turned around and quickly headed for his car.

He climbed in, wiped the sweat from his brow and turned on the ignition.

A minute or two elapsed before Ordway snapped his fingers, anger burning through him. "Son-of-a-bitch, I think we've been suckered!"

"Whaddya mean?" his friend asked, confused.

"I think I know that guy. And I'm damn sure he ain't who he said he was."

"Well, we damn well bettah git aftah him, before he tells the feds about our plans."

***

David nearly reached the main road where a couple of armed men were waiting. They waved him through without any trouble until he looked in the rear-view mirror.

Upon reaching the end of the road, he caught sight of something that made his blood run cold; the sight of a black Dodge Ram a quarter mile behind him.

"Holy shit," he said aloud, "they're following me."

He hadn't gone farther than to the end of a large cornfield when, to his surprise, he found that the road forked.

He had no idea how fast he was going until he peeked down at the speedometer—75, 80, 85, 90.

There were cornfields on both sides of a dirt road that he was crossing. It wasn't a road designed for high speed for any reason.

Should I keep driving or turn onto an access road that might take me in the wrong direction?

He tightened his grip on the steering wheel and pressed his foot down on the brake for control. But the car weaved all over the road, coming to a stop in front of a muddy ditch.

He kicked open his door and raced up a narrow path until he spotted a real estate sign advertising a small cabin for sale.

Not far behind him, he heard someone shout, "Go git 'im, Brutus!"

Upon reaching the cabin, David picked up a brick and broke open a side window.

His heart was racing as he pushed the screen aside. A sharp sting caused by a shard of glass rippled across his hand.

"Shit," he mumbled, looking down at his hand. There was blood running between his fingers but he still managed to boost himself up onto the window ledge so it couldn't have been too bad.

The damp, dark interior of the house was surrounded by a moldy smell.

Where can I hide?

He felt his way across the room and noticed that a small trickle of sunlight lit up a doorway to his right. He hoped that it would take him down to the cellar where he'd hide until help arrived.

He opened the door, stumbled down the stairs and crouched behind the furnace.

His trousers were spattered with mud front and back, and his left hand dripped blood.

He took out his cell phone and attempted to dial 911, but it slipped out of his hand onto the floor.

He heard Ordway and his friend approach from the direction of the stairs. A flashlight rocked slowly to a stop.

His friend held up his hand and pointed at the furnace where David was hiding.

Ordway waved his flashlight in an arc above his head and yelled, "We know where you are so c'mon out. We ain't gonna hurt you!"

He needed to buy more time so he faked his reply, "Go ahead and peek around the corner so I can blow your freaking brains out!"

He looked up and noticed that in the diaphragm valve a thin piece of metal was fixed to an outlet from the boiler. And when moderate pressure is exceeded it would give away, allowing water and steam to escape. Below that was a red warning sign: **DANGER.** *Boiler pressure should not exceed 150 PSI's.*

He turned the handle of the release valve and the pressure slowly began to rise—50, 100, 125—

"If you don't come out by the time I count to ten, we'll come in and git you!" warned Ordway.

"That's big talk for a cowardly, lying son-of-a-bitch!" David shouted back.

He waited until Ordway finished counting before jacking up the handle of the release valve, sending steam, and hot water spewing in their direction.

Blinded by the steam, Ordway screamed, dropped his shotgun and rubbed his eyes. But his friend continued to advance.

The steam created a temporary subterfuge, allowing David to lure him into a trap.

He ducked out of the way, throwing the man off guard as he raised his revolver to fire. But David moved first and swatted the revolver out of his hand.

He turned quickly, jerked an elbow back into the man's stomach and heard his breath escape him in a groan.

The blow was hard enough to bounce him off the back wall. Nearly unconscious, he sat on the floor, glazed eyes open, with a look of stupor on his face.

It's time to get the hell out of here, David thought, stumbling up the stairs and jumping feet first through the broken window.

He vaulted the porch rail, hit the ground running and arrived breathless at the door of his car.

Nearby he could hear mingled vicious snarls and anxious barking.

Fortunately, Ordway's friend had tied Brutus to a tree, making it impossible for him to give chase.

Several seconds later, an explosion blew out the windows of the cabin, sending shards of glass and wood flying across the open field.

He turned on the ignition and backed away from the ditch.

Trees arched over the road, forming a canopy of leaves as he sped away and headed back toward the highway.

A half mile down the road, he spotted flashing lights coming straight toward him. He was startled until he recognized a white Chevy Blazer, the sheriff's car, as it passed him. His reaction turned from concern to a smile.

Once again, he felt lucky to be alive.

He drove straight to a local hospital and had his hand bandaged up.

When he got back to the hotel, he washed the color out of his hair and shaved.

Chapter 38

Alesha arrived home the following day. Leaving her successful tennis thoughts behind and eager to see David, she didn't bother to unpack. Instead, she jumped into her car and raced over to his apartment.

A big surprise awaited her after ringing his doorbell.

The surprise was mutual.

In a few moments, she heard a pleasant female voice ask, "Is that you, Mr. Wellman?"

Alesha was silent for a moment and when she answered, she tried to control the quiver in her voice.

"Ah, no, no—I'm David's girlfriend."

"Hang on a sec, I'll buzz you in," answered Rose, calmly.

While Alesha waited, nothing but pure jealousy guided her thoughts.

Who is this woman, and why is she living in David's apartment?

When Rose opened the door, Alesha's face filled with an intent curiosity.

She gave Rose a hands-on-hips serious look. Standing before her was a woman who looked like a gorgeous movie actor and who oozed sensuality.

Her hair had a satin sheen to it and her skin was tanned a smooth, glossy burnt-orange.

She was splendidly dressed in blues and greens, her elegant shape clad in a very earthly, off-the-shoulder dress, whereas Alesha was dressed in sneakers, torn faded jeans and a light blue sweater.

She gave Rose a nervous wave, watched for her reaction and relieved when she offered a warm smile.

"Hi, I'm Alesha," she said, "and you're—?"

"Rose Gutierrez," she replied, extending her arm for a handshake. "And I know you're surprised to see a stranger living in your boyfriend's apartment."

"Well, ah—yes, I am. Wouldn't you be?"

"I probably would," she answered immediately. "But before you arrive at any conclusion, why don't we both sit down, because what I'm about to say might upset you."

"Even so, that doesn't mean I don't want to know what exactly is going on, especially where David is concerned."

"He's out of town. After I tell you why he left, you must promise not to call him or write him during his absence."

Alesha knitted her eyebrows together. "It's that serious, huh?"

"Yes—serious enough to involve both of us. But you have to understand that I may not be able to explain all the reasons behind his trip."

Confusion flooded Alesha's mind, drowning her in doubt and questions.

"The last time I was with him, all he talked about was getting even with the people whose contemptuous lies sent him to prison."

"Maybe if you and I exchanged stories, it'd help piece together the reason why he brought me here and why he feels so revengeful."

"Before we begin, I'd like to apologize for being so rude. I know it's not your fault that you look so stunning in your clothes."

"You don't have to apologize. Right now, let's just talk about how we can help David solve this mystery."

Chapter 39

Whether Mr. Wellman continued to have any secret communication with the US Government following his retirement, is anyone's guess. There was never any proof of such a connection, but if there was, it served both sides well.

The first was phone-cloning. Using this ingenious method, he was able to intercept incoming messages and send outgoing messages as if they came from his very own phone.

Most of his neighbors thought of him as a peace-loving, law-abiding citizen. He would never use phone-cloning to penetrate their privacy; or seek information by underhanded or unworthy means.

Unless there was a pending crisis of major proportions, telephone messages went unanswered.

However, it was very useful when it came time for David to contact him with some very important information.

Two days had passed since they last talked to each other. And when they finally did, there was genuine uneasiness in David's voice that drew his interest.

"So Ordway and one of his goons chased you and you had to fight your way out of an abandoned cabin?"

"Yeah, and I have a lot to tell you when I get back about a demonstration they plan to hold in Boston."

"Where are you now?"

"I'm still at the hotel."

Mr. Wellman's voice became urgent. "Did you bump into anyone else besides Ordway and his friend?"

"Ah, yes—come to think of it, I did. Two guys were waiting outside the gate when I left."

"This is bad," Mr. Wellman replied, his voice low and quiet. "There's a good chance that they jotted down your car's license number and they'll use it to find you."

"Damn, I never thought about that."

"Where did you rent the car?"

"At the hotel, when I first checked in."

"Pack up and get the hell out of there right now, understand?"

"I'm on my way," David answered without a moment's hesitation.

He began packing up his toiletries when he heard the sound of police sirens.

Seconds later, two cruisers, red lights flashing, pulled up in front of the hotel entrance.

I bet they're looking for me in connection with that explosion. I've got to get out of here.

He peeked out his door to make sure the coast was clear and broke into a quick run.

The exit door was directly in front of him. He made it down to the first floor, where it emptied out into a dark, rainy alley.

His nerves were jumpy and everything around him, people, cars, buses, became a blur.

He stopped, caught his breath, and took some time to center himself and stay calm.

He turned and spotted a small, bearded, wiry man loading laundry hampers into a white box truck.

When he walked back to the hotel's loading dock, David hugged the wall and made his way down the alley, nose wrinkling at the scents of trash and stagnant water.

He jumped into the back of the truck and buried himself beneath a hamper full of soiled linen.

The smell was horrible. He squeezed the upper part of his nose between thumb and index fingers, blinking his eyes to stop the burning.

Soon the driver returned, locked the back door and drove several miles before stopping at another hotel to pick up more linen.

He unlocked the door and almost fainted when David jumped out, pushed him aside, and ran by him.

All he had to do now was get to the Greyhound Bus station and buy a one-way ticket to Boston.

David was tired but happy and a little tense when he finally arrived home.

Alesha crossed her arms and looked at him, meeting his steady look with one of her own.

After he finished his story about what happened in Atlanta, she shook her head and dropped back on the couch.

"Is that all that you've been doing since I left?"

"That's it."

"You've got to stop thinking of yourself as a one man vigilante who thinks he can solve all of this country's problems. Well, you're not."

"I know. But I feel a hell of a lot better knowing Ordway is out of the way and I was able to find out what he and his goons are up to."

"Weren't you afraid of getting hurt?"

"No more than I was when I played football. And as far as this cut on my hand is concerned—it's nothing."

She kissed his injured hand and gently pressed it against her chest.

"While I was away, there were many nights when I thought about how I let my father's stupid prejudice stand between us. I'm glad that I was strong enough to stand up to him."

She felt like they were fully a part of each other when they touched; it was if they had missed more than a piece of each other's souls all these weeks and just now realized it.

"Rose told me how you two met and why she's staying here."

"Yeah—it sounds a little crazy, huh?"

"Not only crazy. But extremely dangerous and that's why I want you to stop doing what you're doing."

What he told Alesha about his close call in Atlanta was unsettling enough, but what he said after that cast a shadow of doubt and insecurity on their relationship.

"I think you know how much I love you, but I still have a lot of work to do," he said.

She shook her head and stared at him, but he didn't look at her.

"So you're not going to stop chasing bad people?" she asked quietly.

"I am, but not right now."

"All the effort your parents put into getting you a college education—don't tell me that you're just going to throw it away."

"What do you want me to say?"

She got tired of not being in full control of their conversation. And his answer sounded like something she had heard before.

"How long do you intend to waste time on something where, as far as I can tell, no one is in danger, whatsoever?"

"I honestly don't know."

"Doesn't it matter at all to you that your doubt is causing problems in our relation—"

He raised his hand and waved it in front of her face. "Listen to me for a second; OK?"

The tone of his voice startled her. She crossed her arms and stiffened for a moment, deciding whether to brush his hand away.

"OK," she replied, sharply.

"While I was in Atlanta, I heard this guy say some things that would scare the crap out of anybody. He stood in front of a large crowd and talked about getting more Nazis and white supremacists to join them when they hold a right wing demonstration in Boston. It sounded to me like a dress rehearsal for something that they're planning to do in the future. Boston is only the beginning."

"If you really want to bring hate groups to justice, don't you think discreet lobbying and law enforcement would be a better way to deal with them?"

"After what happened to me in that courtroom a couple of years ago, it's hard for me to trust another cop?"

She met his regard with equal composer, in spite of the fact that his response was beginning to make her feel extremely uncomfortable.

"C'mon David, you know they're not all alike."

"Maybe not, but those who are don't give a damn what racists do. Because some of them are racists sympathizers and they're the most dangerous of all."

"What about us, David? What am I supposed to do while you run around the country chasing bad people?"

He dropped back on the couch and shrugged his shoulders.

"I wish I knew how to answer that question."

Her voice broke and tears formed in the corner of her eyes. "Don't bother, you just did."

She stood up, turned abruptly and left the room.

For a moment, he was too stunned to say anything.

On her way out, she bumped into Mr. Wellman.

He knew from the troubled look on her face that a problem had just popped up between the two of them.

"Hi Alesha," he said, as she rushed by him.

She didn't reply, but headed straight for her car and turned on the ignition. The engine roared, the tires screeched, and she sped away.

He trotted up the stairs to David's apartment, where he found him staring into space.

"Woman problems, huh?" he asked.

"Yeah—she wants me to stop chasing what she calls '*bad people*'."

"You can stop anytime you want to."

"Yeah, I know."

"If you're upset about what happened in Atlanta, let it go. I've got some information that might make you feel better."

David looked depressed and gloomy. "I hope so."

"One of my contacts has informed me that that guy, *William 'Wimpy' Owens,* who you tangled with last week, has admitted to being a foot soldier for the mafia."

"Really," said David, astounded by Mr. Wellman's disclosure. "How'd he find that out?"

"Apparently, he gave the police enough information to connect Owens to the Amaral crime family in Providence. The FBI has been trying to bring them down for years. Prosecutors are seeking to keep him locked up pending trial because they say he poses a serious flight risk."

"So Rose can go home now."

"No, she can't."

"There's something else going on, huh?"

"There is and it started the minute she entered this apartment."

David sat up straight and shook his head. "Mind telling me what it is?"

"When Owens tried to kidnap her, and you intervened, you became the sole witness to that kidnapping. That makes you somebody the DA would love to talk to, but so far, they don't have any idea who you are. That's why your relationship with her has to remain a secret and why she has to stay here a while longer."

"That's the second time I've screwed things up."

"Not really. Before you left Atlanta, you told me that a number of racists groups are planning to hold a demonstration in Boston. That turned out to be a very hot tip. My contact doesn't exactly know what day that demo is going to happen. But he suspects that someone in town has formed his own small, self-styled militia group. He's been recruiting and organizing members for a demonstration for several months. I was able to intercept several text messages that he sent to a number of neo-Nazi groups who've expressed an interest in joining them."

"At least I got something right."

"Yes, you did. Now it's time for you to realize that tracking bad people is a very dangerous game. It requires discretion and stealth, neither of which are qualities that one might associate with a person as young as you."

David gave him a half-smile.

"It's not half as dangerous as driving around Boston."

Mr. Wellman placed a comforting hand on David's shoulder.

"Listen, stop feeling bad. You did a good job. Oh, by the way, for her own safety, I decided to move Rose into a more secure location."

"How long will she have to stay there?"

"That depends on how long it takes the FBI to decide whether to use her as a witness in the Amaral crime family trial. Her testimony about being kidnapped by one of their thugs and rescued by you wouldn't need corroboration."

"Since I'm still considered a mystery man, I'd like to help you figure out the date that that racists demo is taking place."

"No David, you're through helping us. It's time you started living a normal life."

He began massaging his temples, neck, and forehead, trying to bring complete relief from a tension-filled headache.

"I'm sort of stuck between a rock and a hard place. Lately, I seem to be more interested in chasing bad people than making friends or carving out a future for myself."

"You've been like that for a while now. I think it's time for you to understand why it's so important to have close friends around like Alesha, Chris and Jenny. Without their company, you'll continue to feel that way."

"I guess you're right."

"Chris is coming home for the weekend so why don't you two get together, go out somewhere and have a good time."

"Yeah, we could."

"As for your relationship with Alesha, let things cool down for a few days? I'm quite sure that when you talk to her again, she'll be glad to hear that you've stopped chasing *bad people*. Now I've got to get back to work. Talk to you later."

With so many negative thoughts swirling around in his head, sleep seemed unlikely so he leaned back on the couch; his eyelids fluttered and he fell fast asleep.

What began as a pleasant dream soon turned into a nightmare. He could still hear the frustration in Alesha's voice as she continually tried to talk him out of doing something extremely dangerous.

Not surprisingly, he could see his own black memories playing on the screens on the back of his eyelids; sitting alone in a jail cell at Danbury Prison.

Half of his face was stuck in the shadows, giving him a surreal appearance, as if he had one foot in a confused world; the other in a world filled with desperation and despair.

Then he heard Mr. Wellman's relaxing voice, "Your parents are and always will be your best friends. They helped you regulate your emotions, gave you a positive outlook on life, and supported you when you needed it. I don't think you ever got over losing them."

***

The next morning the sun rose bright; the sky without a cloud.

David awoke convinced that his nightmare was caused by exhaustion.

He stretched and flexed his knees to relax himself before turning on the TV.

A reporter's face appeared on the screen. His report immediately caught David's attention.

"Waltham Police have issued an appeal for help after an unidentified man fled an attempted kidnapping scene two days ago with a woman identified as 35-year-old Rose Gutierrez."

"We're doing anything and everything, turning this city upside down to find them," said Police Chief Michael Kaplan.

"Concern is growing, from across the state, over her whereabouts and well-being," he said.

"Gutierrez was last seen at her home at 120 Lakeview Terrace shortly after midnight Wednesday."

"An investigation is continuing."

He walked into the front room and peeked through the blinds, expecting to see someone lurking across the parking lot.

The only person he spotted was Chris Wellman, polishing his 2010 Dodge Charger.

Good, Chris is home. I'll tell him what I've been doing the last few months and why it's causing problems between me and Alesha. He's my quarterback. He'll tell me what to do.

Chapter 40
7 AM, the Day Before

Following her meeting with David, Alesha drove straight home. A lump had formed in her throat and tears continued to spill from her eyes.

She'd have a lot of explaining to do if her parents saw her crying. So she decided to walk through the kitchen to reach the stairs rather than cross through the living room.

The hallway was quiet except for the hollow and remorseless tick of a grandfather clock in the corner.

Before she reached the stairwell, she saw a dark figure duck into her father's study, followed by several voices, both distinctly male. One of them belonged to her father, the other sounded vaguely familiar.

She stared at the study door for a moment, curious as to why a stranger would call on her father so early in the morning.

The door was slightly ajar so she peeked inside and caught sight of her father, who was engaged in a hushed conversation with Detective Sergeant Karl Toomey.

The terrible things she overheard made her immediately forget herself and her own grief.

"Our recruiting drive in Atlanta got off to a fast start," said Toomey. "But it bogged down right after Ordway thought he recognized someone who might have been spying on us. He wanted to keep our plan secret so when the guy split, he chased him. That's when he got hurt."

"Did he get the guy's name?"

"Bennie, Bennie Franklin from Boston."

"Is there any possibility of finding out who he *really* is?"

"If I do, he'll regret the day he was born."

"Where's Ordway now?"

"He and his buddy are still in the hospital. They're expected to be there for a couple of days."

"It looks like Mr. Franklin is extremely dangerous. If that's his real name, he's thrown a monkey wrench into our plans."

"That's too bad because a lot of people were looking forward to joining us."

"Not everyone understands the price that comes with being a patriot these days. So after you leave here, call the President of the Springfield Proud Boys chapter and tell him that we might have to change the date of our demonstration in Boston. Let him know that his gifts, his thoughts, and his financial contributions will help us take this country back," the judge replied.

"Yes, sir."

Suddenly, Alesha thought she heard a rustling noise that startled her. She turned quickly and was greeted with a big smile from her mother, who had hardly made any sound descending the stairs.

"Welcome home, darling. How was your trip?" she said, loud enough for her husband and Toomey to hear.

Judge Cross pressed his index finger against his lips and waved his hand in front of Toomey's face to discontinue their conversation. Then he stood up and stepped into the hall.

"Good morning Alesha," he said, opening his arms wide; hugging her. "I'm glad that you got home safely. You must be very tired."

She returned his hug with less enthusiasm. "Yeah, I guess I'm suffering from jet-lag."

"We have a lot to talk about," her mother said. "I'll have breakfast sent up to your room and you can grab a nap. You'll feel better afterwards."

"That's a good idea. I hate to leave such good company, but I'm so tired I can hardly keep my eyes open."

She glanced at her father, wondering why he was eyeing her, a wry smile twisting his lips.

"See you around noon," she said, kissing her mother on the cheek.

While ascending the stairs, she thought she heard someone mention her name.

The hostility in his voice and expression was unnerving.

She quickened her step and her breath came in spurts as she gingerly climbed the stairs and entered her room.

Everything that that guy said to my father is very similar to what David told me. He's in trouble, so I've got to warn him.

She fumbled around in her pocketbook for her cell phone. It wasn't there.
"What the hell is wrong with me?" she said aloud, banging her hand down on the bed. "Everything—my cell phone and my laptop are in my backpack!"
At the same time, another troubling thought entered her mind.

If I go downstairs right now to get it, they'll know I'm up to something. I'll just have to be patient until the coast is clear.

Suddenly, tension and fatigue signaled that it was time to rest.
She flopped back on the bed, covered her eyes with one arm and fell asleep.

Chapter 41
Present Day

Rose Gutierrez was nervous. Two days had passed since she last saw Bill and she began to wonder if his health had improved.

She was comfortable in Mr. Wellman's basement apartment but it was boring and without color, a real man's cave where they did nothing more than drink beer, watch football, and sleep.

The question of how much longer she'd have to stay there was answered in a late breaking news story.

Waltham police may be one step closer today in solving the disappearance of a 35-year-old Puerto Rican woman.

Moments ago, a receptionist at the Whitman Rehab Center told police a woman that she identified as Rose Guttierez visited one of their patients earlier in the day. Minutes later, two men, one of them identified as 45-year-old William 'Wimpy' Owens, asked to see the same patient.

The receptionist explained, in nervous little spurts, how she heard the news of Guttierez's disappearance.

She also told police that she might be able to identify the second man from a composite sketch they're putting together.

Guttierez was last seen three days ago when Owens allegedly tried to kidnap her.

According to her landlord, the unidentified man confronted Owens and was able to rescue her.

He and Guttierez vanished and haven't been seen or heard from since.

A few seconds later, she heard footsteps outside her door. The doorknob rattled, someone tried to open it.

"ROSE!" Mr. Wellman called out. "If you're decent, open the door. I have to talk to you."

"Just a minute," she said, slipping on a bathrobe.

She opened the door. He entered and closed it behind himself.

"Sorry to bother you," he said, his eyes shifting from her face to the TV, "but it looks like another big problem just popped up."

"Yeah, I just saw the same story and it looks like I'm it."

"No, you're not."

"I don't understand."

"I'm a sympathetic old fool. And because Bill Parham had a relationship with David's mother, I sent him to the hospital to check on his condition. He had no way of knowing that you and Owens would be there. I blame myself for everything that happened afterwards."

"My father once told me that sometimes you have to praise enemies and blame friends."

"What he said makes a whole lot of sense."

She cocked her head to one side and gave him a questioning look.

"It does?"

"Yes," he replied. "And it's time to make some sense out of everything that's happened over the past couple of weeks."

"How can I help?"

"On the back of that business card that Mr. Parham carried, someone scribbled the initials ANP, a telephone number, a swastika and a whole lot of other crap. We already know ANP stands for the American Nazi Party and the swastika is their symbol for hatred and fear. The same day that his name and face appeared in newspapers and on TV, that telephone was disconnected."

Rose rubbed her chin and thought.

"It sounds very suspicious to me."

"It is. And since he's still alive, you might be the only person who can figure out who that telephone number belonged to."

"If I try to see him, the police are going to catch me and send me back to Puerto Rico. And what if there are more people out there who want to hurt me?" she said, fear clutching at her throat.

"Take a deep breath and relax," he said. "I've already notified the FBI that you're here. They want you to stay put, so don't worry."

"Are you sure?"

"Yes. And as far as the police are concerned, the FBI wants to use your disappearance as a subterfuge."

"Will I still be able to talk to Bill?"

"Yes, and from now on you're going to talk to him directly from here," he answered, picking up the remote and tuning in to a private channel.

The left side of his computer keyboard contained a layout, similar to a typewriter's, only with additional function keys along the top. Starting up the computer, he pulled up a word program and typed something.

She looked at him with a puzzled frown.

"No lo entiendo. I don't get it."

"Not everyone realizes that television is and should remain the last bastion of the desperate," he said. "And since we're both desperate, I'm going to use Advanced Computer Technology to hook us up with Bill Parham."

She still looked confused so he thought of a better way to explain.

"When I worked for the government, I used a similar system to track down Nazis. It was effective. But it was also very complicated. This morning, I installed a newly designed chip that should simplify things," he said, watching the screen flicker and then light up.

"How do you know it'll work?"

"I don't, but I think it's worth a try," he answered.

A few seconds later, Bill Parham's face appeared. He looked comfortable, sitting in a wheelchair, hands folded in his lap.

Standing on one side of him was Dr. Corrado. On the other side, an FBI agent.

Seeing him caused her face to beam with delight.

"This is amazing!" she said loudly, wiggling her fingers at them.

"Hi Rose," Dr. Corrado said, with a casual wave. "Nice seeing you again. I'm here today with FBI Agent Mike Kay. Thanks to you, Mr. Parham has had an amazing recovery one that has confounded both me and my colleagues."

"I'm glad I could help," she said, overjoyed to see a slight smile spread across Bill's lips, a twinkle in his eyes.

"Apparently, the song that you sang to him several months ago helped stimulate parts of his brain," Dr. Corrado explained. "So today, we attached electrodes to his body and we're asking you to sing it again."

"You mean Bésame Mucho?" she asked.

"That song appears to have affected his auditory cortex, which we in the medical field consider the gateway for music," he explained. "It also helped to stimulate his cerebellum when he heard it."

"That's great!" she said excitedly.

"Let's just hope it works. Mr. Wellman will take over from here."

"I'm going to use a Digital Translator System to decipher what Mr. Parham hears into alphabets or numbers," he explained. "While you're singing, I'll say one of those numbers or letters that someone jotted down on the back of that card. For example, the first letter in the alphabet is A. My computer will convert it to one. The second numeral is two. My computer will convert it to B and vice-versa."

"OK, I'm ready?" she said eagerly.

"We're going to move slowly so we don't over stimulate his brain," he said, nodding his head for her to begin.

In a voice that sounded a bit nervous, she began to sing. *Bésame Bésame Mucho. Hold me, my darling, and say that you'll always be mine. Bésame, Bésame Mucho. Each time I cling to your kiss I hear music divine—*

Bill Parham sat silent for a moment, nodding his head slowly while Mr. Wellman read all the numbers and letters on the back of the card, pausing briefly between each one. "A-5125-BO F-A-G-C-E-H-D-I-A-C."

Rose's full, rich singing voice filled the room. And in a matter of minutes, all of the decoded information popped up on Mr. Wellman's computer screen: **1 May 20, 617 358 4913**

"Our office believes someone used that telephone number to relay messages to everyone who plans to join a racist demonstration in Boston on that date," FBI Agent Kay said. "It coincides with the alarming increase of excess chatter intercepted a week ago by our telephone tracking system. None lasted more than six seconds, making it impossible to trace."

"Apparently, the caller used a Dark Web browser to obtain a false Internet Protocol address. Once he had that, all he had to do is use a series of relays to mask his identity," Mr. Wellman said. "What we have to do now is figure out who that person is and stop them from spreading terrorism and preaching violence."

Suddenly Bill began to mutter unceasingly, his eyebrows and lips twitching, and it was impossible to tell whether he understood what was going on around him or not.

Rose looked seriously concerned about the toll the session had exerted on him.

"I think he's had enough for now so we're going to take him back to his room so he can rest," Dr. Corrado said.

"Will he be alright?" she asked.

"Don't worry, he'll be fine," he answered, detaching the sensors from around Bill's head. "Give me a call later today and I'll update you on his condition."

"Thanks Mr. Wellman," Agent Kay said. "Once again, you've been a big help. It may take a day or two to identify the person who owned that telephone, but I'm sure we'll find him."

From the amount of information that David gave to Mr. Wellman about Atlanta, he suspected the person was either a neo-Nazi or a member of a racist organization.

Their propensity for violence and extremism was no secret to him. In the past, the FBI and other agencies had often seen them as nothing more than mere street brawlers who lacked the organization or ambition of typical bureau targets like international terrorists, and Mexican drug cartels. A lot of things have changed since then.

He glanced at Rose, who still had a concerned look on her face. "It makes everything you just heard a bit suspect doesn't it?"

"Do you think Bill made any of those calls?" she asked.

"No, but I think he knows the name of the person who did."

"I'll be glad to sing Bésame Mucho again if that'll help," she said innocently.

FBI Agent Kay gave her a warm smile. "Thanks, but right now that won't be necessary. I want to assure both of you, however, that our agency is committed to using every means necessary to disrupt that person from creating violence, including hate-fueled attacks on innocent people."

Chapter 42

Lightning flashed brilliantly and thunder rattled the windowpanes in their frames, the sound loud enough to wake Alesha out of a deep sleep. She glanced at her watch, surprised to see that she had napped for three hours.

"Holy shit!" she said aloud, jumping up from her bed and rubbing the sleep from her eyes.

"I've got to get my cell phone so I can warn David that he's in big trouble."

Lightning flashed again so bright that the entire room lit up. Shortly after, it thundered loud enough to make the room shudder.

It scared her; but not half as much as when she thought she saw a man in a dark suit leave her room.

She assumed it was the butler, who had placed a tray of food down on her night table.

A suspicion entered her mind. She reached over and turned on the lamp to take a closer look.

Suddenly the lights flickered, the power went off, darkness engulfed the entire room.

She picked up her pocketbook and fumbled around in the dark.

Something was missing.

"Now what the hell did I do with my car keys?" she mumbled.

She dug through the pockets of her jeans, pulled out some wrinkled dollar bills, but still no keys. Frantically checking her coat pocket, she came up with what she expected—nothing.

Whoever was in my room a few minutes ago, took them, she thought, a general unease beginning to set in.

The seconds literally ticked away on the old grandfather clock downstairs. She had to make her move now, while the house was quiet.

She quietly opened the door to her room, carefully closed it behind her and took a deep breath.

By the time she reached the bottom of the stairs, tiny flecks of lightning began to dance across her vision.

Quick steps came toward her behind a bobbing flashlight.

Thinking it might be a burglar, she looked toward the garage, concerned that she hadn't heard a car or a door motor yet.

She felt the hair rising on the back of her neck as the footsteps got closer. That's when she and her father nearly bumped into each other.

The look of fright on her face was immediately picked up by him.

She shielded her eyes from the glare and said, "You scared me half to death."

He stood sleepy and frowning, gray hair tousled, his dark eyes studying her intently.

"You didn't plan to hide out here because you're afraid of the storm, did you?" he asked gruffly.

Her mouth felt dry, her voice barely a whisper. "No—I was so tired when I got home today I may have left my phone and my laptop in my backpack."

He gazed at her with mock surprise.

"It looks like I'm the only one with a flashlight, c'mon, I'll help you find it."

He shined his flashlight on her car, her fingers found the door handle and she tugged at it.

"I don't remember locking the door," she said, her hands beginning to perspire.

"Where's your spare key?"

"Mom has it," she replied, her heart racing; her breath coming quickly.

"She'll be out of town for a couple of days, so you'll have to wait until she gets back. If you don't have any plans to go out tonight, I'll get a locksmith over here tomorrow."

She looked over the top of her car and expressed her approval, but her mind was consumed with suspicion.

"Thanks, I'm in no hurry."

"Good," he said calmly, avoiding her eyes as he walked past her. "Till then you should eat something, catch up on your studies, and rest."

He's playing another mind game. But I have no other choice than to go along with it.

After she returned to her room, she wondered if he knew all along what she was thinking.

Right now, all she wanted was someone to talk to. But she couldn't share what she heard earlier in the day with nobody except David. And the last time they talked, he wasn't listening.

Chapter 43

Whenever Alesha returned from a tennis tournament, the first things she'd do is call Jenny.

They called it *'girl talk'*—actually nothing more than tiny bits of gossip that they didn't have to share with anyone. This time, the call that Jenny expected never came.

Either her flight was canceled or she missed it altogether, so she called her.

She was surprised that the ringing on her phone went unanswered, but at least it hadn't been disconnected.

Meantime, David turned toward Chris, in sore need of a pep talk as only his best friend could provide.

The dining room at Wellman's was nearly full so they decided to sit in a quiet corner and chat.

"I asked Jenny to join us," said Chris. "I bet she'll have some good advice on how you and Alesha can get back together."

"I don't know if anything is going to work. She was really pissed at me because of my decision to track down—"

"Hold on a sec, there she is now," said Chris, holding up his hand and waving it in her direction.

"Hi guys," she said, dropping into her chair. "Has either one of you talked to Alesha since she got back?"

"Yeah, I did a couple of hours ago," answered David. "Why'd you ask?"

"Mmm—that's strange. She usually calls me as soon as she gets home. This time she didn't, so I called her. Her phone rang, but she never answered."

"Maybe I pissed her off so much that she needs a couple of days to unwind."

Jenny seemed puzzled, her dark brows drawing together questioningly.

"I always thought you two were the perfect match."

"Yeah—so did I until tonight."

Her gaze ran over his troubled face. "What happened?"

He sighed in exasperation. "She thinks I've made some bad decisions."

"Maybe you have—especially the one about getting even with criminals?"

"How'd you know about that?"

"Women are different than men. We like to *discuss* things. Before her last trip, we talked a lot about you. She was a little upset about the way you've been acting."

Her verbal slap stunned him. Suddenly, he felt that revenge was not the only thing that would make him whole again. Alesha meant more to him than anything else, and he wasn't about to give her up.

"Damn it!" he blurted out. "She was right. There are other ways to deal with bad people. So I'm going to call her right after dinner and apologize for not listening to what she said."

Chris cleared his throat to get their attention.

"OK—now that our sub QB has solved your problem, I'm starving. So whaddya say we order something to eat?"

Chapter 44

As soon as David entered his apartment, he heard his phone ring. He nearly tripped as he dashed across the room to answer. He thought it was Alesha but when he answered, all he heard was someone's quick breathing—loud in his ears.

"Hello, hello. Who's calling?" he asked. "Is anyone there?"

Click—whoever it was, hung up.

Someone must have butt-dialed me.

However, he was eager to tell her about his decision to stop chasing 'bad people' and concentrate more on their building a future together.

He called her twice and each time he was unable to reach her, so he left a message asking for her forgiveness.

His unanswered calls went directly to her voice mail.

He plopped down on the sofa, picked up the remote and tuned into Channel 7 late news.

"This story just in," said the anchor:

A neo-Nazi group called 'The Base' is reportedly planning a demonstration this weekend in Boston. According to law enforcement officials, a number of hate groups are flying in from around the country to join them. In a statement, a State Police spokesperson says troopers are prepared to help with security operations and directing crowds and traffic. Anyone who participates in any kind of violent activity during the planned demonstration will be arrested and prosecuted to the full extent of the law. If there are threats, we will charge those as well.

"In other news—"

Everything David heard during his trip to Atlanta was becoming a reality.

There was still one missing link. Nobody knew the name of the person responsible for organizing the demonstration.

And he didn't want to get involved again in tracking down that individual. But in truth, he was still involved with the past.

He turned off the TV and shook his head in an attempt to stop more revengeful thoughts from entering his mind.

Alesha was more important to him and he realized how much he loved her.

Maybe she'd call him back before the night was over.

An hour earlier

It was nearly midnight before Jenny left the restaurant and headed home. On her way, she tried to call Alesha again. But all she heard this time was a busy signal.

Overcome by curiosity, she decided to drop by Alesha's house to see if she was alright. What she wanted was to do was see Alesha's face. That would put her fears to rest.

The wheels of her car crunched on gravel as she stopped in front of the garage.

She looked in both directions down the pristine, eerily quiet driveway and let out a long sigh.

Everything was dark except for the curtains on the first floor.

Maybe they left them open because of the power outage to allow the moon to shine in.

Not far away, a man stood in the shadows, watching her.

She was ready to turn off the ignition when she heard heavy footsteps approach her car.

Something smashed her side window with a loud crash, the impact causing bits of shattered glass to scatter across her lap. To avoid serious injury, she instinctively covered her head with both hands.

Someone grabbed them with a grip that drove the blood from her fingertips. Using his other hand, he reached inside and tried to open the door.

She screamed, "Get the fuck away from me!" batting at him while trying to escape.

When he didn't release his grip, she sunk her teeth into his wrist.

"Aaahh! You fucking bitch!" he howled in pain, struggling to pull his hand away.

She pressed her foot down hard on the accelerator, the car lurched forward, the sight and scent of his blood already making her want to vomit.

Feet dragging along the gravel, he crooked his left arm over the door and desperately tried to hang on until she used her left foot to kick him away.

She was driving so fast the breeze blowing in through the broken window caught the loose hair hanging down her shoulders. Thick strands of it blew into her eyes, blinding her for a few seconds. She brushed it away just in time to avoid crashing into the water fountain.

The road ahead of her was clear, except for one big truck coming her way, a car approaching the exit to her right.

She looked in the rear-view mirror and quickly accessed her options.

Relieved to see that no one had chased her, she avoided both of them by pulling into a nearby rest stop.

So shaken by the encounter, she dropped her head down on the steering wheel, became hysterical and started to cry.

Chapter 45

Because of his significant computer experience, Mr. Wellman was invited to attend a meeting with law enforcement officials to discuss security plans for the upcoming May Day celebration.

They sought the meeting after members of a neo-Nazi group gathered last year along the parade route and disrupted the event that left forty people injured, five of them seriously.

They hoped to keep that from happening again.

He was led down a long corridor at FBI Headquarters to a large conference room filled with city officials, some standing and sitting, some taking notes. Others had their eyes fastened on computer screens.

The main floor exhibited three offices that were stocked with multiple secure computers.

FBI Agent Kay met him there and greeted him with a strong handshake. "Sorry to get you up so early but a lot of interesting things have happened since I last talked to you."

"Don't you folks ever go to bed?" Mr. Wellman asked.

"Yeah, we do, except when we have to gather enough information, that'll tell us more than we already know."

"I'll help you as much as I can," he said, sitting down in front of a computer, his name jotted down on a piece of masking tape stuck to the back of his chair.

Agent Kay sat down beside him.

"Last night, my boss gave me permission to use a secret-level classified system to intercept several incoming messages from a racist organization," he said. "One message stood out above all the others. Someone in the American Nazi Party downloaded an app that allows a cell phone to operate like a push-to-talk walkie-talkie."

"It sounds like they plan to use their cell phone to connect with a command control center where information can be accessed remotely."

"Less than an hour later," Agent Kay said, "someone else used that same phone to alert racist organizations to bring respirators, masks, snow goggles, knee pads and baseball helmets to the May Day celebration."

"It sounds like a nightmare waiting to happen," Mr. Wellman said, staring at the computer screen.

"Let me assure you that the FBI and local authorities are going to do everything in their power to see that it *doesn't* happen."

Mr. Wellman blew on his fingers to warm them up. Then he tapped on the keyboard.

"I just hope that whoever downloaded that app used a PC to do it. That'll make it easier for me to access all of the information on their computer and their smart phone to see what's happening."

Five different computer programs popped up on the screen. He rested his cursor on the third one and clicked the mouse.

"The first thing I'm going to do is download a program that'll allow me to play a game similar to chess. It's called *Checkmate*."

"Sounds good to me," said Agent Kay.

Mr. Wellman's game continued for the next hour until he found what he was looking for.

"Hate groups often send e-mails the same way spam is sent, by sending them from *innocent* computers."

"So that's why we had trouble cutting off their transmissions, huh?"

"More than likely," Mr. Wellman answered. "The most effective way to physically destroy an adversary's computer or critical network nodes is to create a virus that'll make all of their devices inoperable. However, I need your permission to use it."

"You have it."

He pointed his finger at the screen. "Right now, someone in a local neo-Nazi organization is using the app to make calls and input data. This is where *Checkmate* comes in," he said, clicking the mouse twice. "Unlike mainstream pugilism, fighters can win by knocking out their opponents, but in this case, we're going to win using *Checkmate*."

"So you plan to erase all the data on their hard drive, huh?"

"Similar, except I'm not going to delete their app, I'm just going to clog it up. From now on, whenever someone tries to use it, *Checkmate* will shut them down. If they try to use it again within ten seconds, their computer will crash."

"Pretty damned ingenious," Agent Kay said.

"Sometimes computer viruses can be very helpful," Mr. Wellman said brightly.

Chapter 46

Someone had breached Jenny's comfort zone in a way that left her shaken, scared and extremely angry.

But if Alesha had at least one friend with a sassy personality and a brave and determined heart, it was Jenny. And she wasn't about to let last night's incident slip through the cracks.

"I'm telling you guys something strange is going on at Alesha's house. If you don't believe me, take a look at my car window," she said, her voice trembling.

"You're lucky that you weren't seriously injured?" said Chris, looking at the shattered glass spread across the front seat of her car. "Where you able to get a good look at whoever who did that?"

"It was dark and all the lights in her driveway were off."

"David paced back and forth, deep in thought and extremely concerned about Alesha."

"You're not planning to go back to her house by yourself, are you?" he asked.

Jenny didn't think there was any reason to wait. "What the hell would you do if you were in my place?" she asked, directing an angry scowl at him.

"I certainly wouldn't return to the scene of the crime because you'd have a hard time trying to prove that what happened to you, actually happened there."

"Look—I'm only here to help. If it's not appreciated—then lotsa luck, guys," she replied.

"It's not like we don't believe you," said Chris. "It's more like having enough proof to make that person pay for breaking your car window and assaulting you."

"I would if I saw his wrist, because I bit the shit out of it," she said.

Suddenly something that Mr. Wellman told David several months ago, popped into his brain.

He will win who knows when to fight and when not to fight—A quote from Sun Tzu's book, the *Art of War.*

"Hold on," he said, raising his hand to get their attention. "Neither one of us has heard from Alesha since she got home, right? And someone last night must've had a good reason to scare the hell out of Jenny."

Chris chimed in. "Elementary, my good man—to keep Alesha from communicating with us, all they had to do is confiscate her cell phone and her laptop—completely cutting her off from the outside world. What happened to Jenny was nothing more than a scare tactic."

Jenny snapped her fingers. "See, I knew I was right! Something strange is going on at her house. And I'd like to know what the hell it is."

"We all would," said David. "So let's come up with a plan that'll tell us exactly what it is."

"What do you have in mind?" she asked.

"Since you're Alesha's best friend, I assume you've been to her house a couple of times."

"I have, quite a few times, especially on her birthday."

"I need to know the exact location of her bedroom and what you remember about the surrounding area."

"It's in the back of the house on the second floor. It overlooks a fenced-in tennis court. Her room is the only one there with a balcony. There's a golf course about thirty-five—maybe forty feet away."

He looked at Chris. "Have you still got that great arm?"

"Yeah—I think so. Why'd you ask?" he inquired, wondering what was going on inside David's head.

"I'm going to write a simple message to Alesha on one of my souvenir footballs," David answered. "All you have to do is land it right in the center of Alesha's balcony. Think you can do that?"

Chris was unsure how to respond. "There are two things you may have forgotten, footballs bounce off of hard surfaces. And it all depends on where I'm standing when I throw it."

"Make believe there's only three seconds left on the clock and we're behind by two points," said David, maintaining a positive outlook. "What would you do?"

"You know exactly what I'd do. I'd go for the touchdown."

"Right, just like we did a couple of years ago."

"OK, you got me," Chris answered. "I'll give it a try. But don't blame me if I miss."

***

The sky turned dark, heavy with clouds, when they decided to put David's plan into motion.

They took a hilly and scenic route across the golf course and ended up behind a six foot high chain-link fence.

Chris and David crouched low. Jenny followed closely behind.

When they stopped to reconnoiter the area, she pointed at Alesha's room.

"There it is," she whispered.

Using his high-powered binoculars, David measured an angular deviation of 40–50 feet from where they were standing to her balcony.

"Think you can reach it?" he asked.

Chris shrugged his shoulders. "I don't know. There's not a lot of wind so I'll give it a fifty-fifty chance."

Jenny squinted and peered through her fingers.

"I don't want to see this. Just let me know when it's over."

Chris pressed his left foot down on the grass to test its firmness, stretched his arms and took a deep breath. Within seconds, he exhaled.

He took three steps back and cocked his arm. As soon as the football left his hand, they waited in silence and prayed that it would land on Alesha's balcony.

A couple of minute earlier, something distracted Brutus, and he started barking.

The sound awakened Alesha from a light nap. She stood up, walked over to the balcony door and opened it.

When he growls or barks like that, something outside has disturbed him, she thought.

A football whizzed by her ear, ricocheted off her bedroom wall, bounced around on the floor several times before coming to rest near her bed.

For a moment, she was dumbfounded, too startled to do anything but stare at it.

"Holy shit!" she said aloud, before noticing that someone had used a white magic marker to scribble a message on it.

Trouble—raise 1 arm.
No trouble—raise 2
Luv—David

Tears flooded her eyes as she stepped out onto the balcony. She wiped them away with her left hand and signaled to him with her right.

She held it up for a few seconds before slowly lowering it. Then she placed both hands over her chest and formed a heart-shaped symbol, a sign that she was still deeply in love with him.

David kept his binoculars trained on her until she signaled that someone was knocking on her door. "We'd better get the hell out of here before whoever it is sees us," he whispered.

Beneath the cover of the surrounding trees, they scrambled out of the golf course and back to the main road.

"Alesha, Alesha!" her father called out. "I just heard a strange noise coming from your room. Are you alright?"

She hid the football under her bed, and answered, "Just a second, I'll be right there."

As soon as she opened the door, his eyes circled the room. He stepped out onto the balcony and looked out over the tennis court.

"Something must have disturbed Brutus. He's been barking for quite a while."

"He barks at everything. Don't worry, he'll calm down soon. I just hope he didn't scare the locksmith away."

"Oh, I meant to tell you that he was here while you were napping. We looked everywhere for your backpack. Are you sure you didn't leave it at the airport?"

"I'm positive," she answered, the edge of desperation in her voice.

"If you attached a tag with your name, address, and telephone number on it, I'm quite sure it'll show up in a day or two."

"Dad, you don't seem to understand. My cell phone and my laptop are inside my backpack and I need them *right now*."

"They can be replaced, so calm down," he said, trying to avoid her angry gaze.

She wanted to tell him to take a long walk off a short pier; instead, she brazenly stepped in front of him.

"I hope you don't mind if I ask you a very important question."

"No—not at all," he answered nervously.

"You've kept Mom and me in the dark for quite a while, so I think it's time for you to tell us what the hell is going on?"

"You're stubborn, suspicious of everyone, and you ask so many damn stupid questions," he replied, feeling intimidated, a stress headache coming on.

His face turned red so she thought it best to step aside and let him leave. "Never mind—I don't want to cause your blood pressure to go up."

"Look, I'm sorry," he said, "I didn't mean to yell at you. It's just that I have a lot of things on my mind right now."

"I understand."

"I have an early appointment at the courthouse tomorrow morning. You can go with me. Then my driver can drop you off at Circuit City, where you can buy a brand new computer and a cell phone. How does that sound?"

"OK Dad," she answered, realizing it was too late to warn David that there was trouble ahead.

Chapter 47
8:00 AM

The following morning Alesha awoke and thought she heard her father talking to someone. She got up and peeked over the banister. The caller's voice was gruff, and he spoke very fast. However, she couldn't hear what he was saying or what he looked like.

She had a slight headache and thought it might have something to do with the tension-filled conversation she had with her father the night before.

She blinked her bleary eyes and called out to him. "Dad, who are you talking too?"

"I'm sorry if I disturbed you but I had to sign for a special delivery of my blood pressure medicine from Wellman's," he replied. "My doctor must have reordered them for me."

His answer revealed something that gave her pause for thought.

Blood pressure pills from Wellman's. I'll bet David came up with that idea.

Her father appeared to be in a hurry. "Alesha, I'm leaving in a half hour. Are you still planning to go with me?"

"Yes," she answered, "I'll be down in a couple of minutes."

"Good, because I have a meeting to attend. So if you don't mind, my driver will drop you off at the Circuit City store where you can buy whatever you need. We'll pick you up back there in about an hour. How does that sound?"

She looked down at him, her expression quizzical. "Thanks, Dad. Mind if I use your credit card? Mine are all in my backpack."

"No, I don't mind at all, just don't lose it."

Chapter 48
9:00 AM, An Hour
Before the May Day Celebration

Alesha stepped into the Circuit City store just as a large group of racists gathered on Boston Common waving American and Confederate flags, using bull horns and cowbells to attract attention.

Less than a block away, a vocal group of demonstrators from the neo-Nazi party began roaming the street, scornful of police or security guards who were trying to protect businesses in downtown Boston.

On the opposite side of the street, a Black Lives Matter march was about to begin.

The protesters were reluctant to leave the Common and more police arrived dressed in riot gear carrying tear gas canisters and batons.

Not very often do opposing groups like this come face to face with each other. But when they do, emotions can rise to volatile levels. Within an hour, that's exactly what happened.

A neo-Nazi, wearing a cross around his neck, a bandanna covering his face, spoke to supporters through a megaphone. His strong, hateful words stirred up the crowd just enough to turn them into a violent mass of humanity.

He received pushback from counter-protesters, who blew whistles and chanted at him to "Go home!"

Protesters threatened and insulted each other and soon they resembled one body, pushing, shoving, and screaming at each other.

Boston police pushed through the crowd, doing their best to keep both groups separated.

For Alesha, the situation was becoming extremely dangerous.

People who were planning to go sightseeing could hardly step out of their hotel before being pelted with refuse, and neo-Nazi's yelling obscenities.

It wasn't easy, but fortunately David had enough strength and maneuverability to push his way through the crowd before someone threw a rock smashing open the storefront window.

Inside, Alesha and a dozen other customers ducked behind counters or hit the floor to avoid being showered with glass.

David rushed inside and wrapped his arms around her waist. "Stay put," he said, hugging her close to his body, "I'm going to get you out of here."

She couldn't remember anything as comforting as his protective strength and comforting words.

"Where's the exit?" he asked a salesperson.

Teeth chattering, too frightened to talk, he pointed toward the rear of the building.

"OK everyone, keep your heads down and follow me!" David shouted.

Alesha held his hand tightly. The rest of the customers followed them out the exit door and onto the main street where Chris and Jenny waited patiently.

"Thank god, you're safe," she said, giving Alesha a big hug.

"How'd you know I'd be here?" she asked.

"That was David's idea. After you signaled us that you were in trouble, we decided to follow you this morning. It was Chris who delivered that package of medicine to your father."

"We'd better get going. The longer we stay here, the harder it's going to be to get back to the car," he said.

They slipped in among the demonstrators to avoid being noticed by a speaker who was now on the Common, spouting a litany of racist rhetoric and grievances.

Those who listened were part of the same group that had planned their demonstration in Atlanta and expected to return home triumphant. Some of them appeared to be armed and dangerous.

From one end of the Common to the other everything grew extremely loud, with voices jumbling, the sound of police sirens and the thump of a State Police helicopter overhead.

In that tense moment, David was certain he recognized someone. Half of his face was hidden behind a kerchief, but his silver-white hair was too familiar to be anyone else's.

His expression revealed surprise for a brief second, then they flashed with anger. "It's that lying cop, Toomey," he muttered beneath his breath.

"Are you sure?" asked Chris, opening the back door of his car to let Jenny and Alesha climb in.

"I'd know that son-of-a-bitch anywhere," he answered, suddenly feeling more like the hunter than the prey. But amid all of the confusion, he lost sight of him.

"David, don't leave me, please don't leave me again," Alesha pleaded, grabbing his arm and holding on tightly.

His gaze was steady and commanding as he sought to connect with her panicked mind. "Don't worry baby, I'm not going anywhere."

She didn't release her grip until he climbed in beside her and gave her a big hug, along with a flutter of butterfly kisses across her face.

Chris's eyes flickered toward the rear-view mirror as he pulled his car away from the curb.

"I'm glad we're getting the hell out of here. The whole Common is beginning to look like a battleground."

"Yeah, and Alesha almost got caught in the middle of it," Jenny said. "What I'm trying to figure out is why her father dropped her off an hour before the demonstration began."

Alesha looked at David with fear and said, "He knew exactly what he was doing. That's what I was trying to warn you about yesterday, but someone took my phone so I had no way of contacting you."

"Everything is beginning to add up," he replied. "I'll bet it's the same person who broke Jenny's window."

A lengthy silence followed while Alesha recalled the conversation she overheard between her father and Toomey.

How deeply involved is my father in planning the demonstration?

"Take me home," she said abruptly, feeling that he had planted the seed of distrust in her mind. "I have a good idea where my backpack is."

Upon arrival, David followed her as she ran to the courtyard and slipped in through the back door.

She headed to her father's office, then stopped and listened.

"Good, nobody's here. You look in that file cabinet next to the closet, and I'll look in his desk."

It took her less than five minutes to find what she was looking for. Stuffed inside a cardboard mailing box beneath his desk was her backpack.

She opened her mouth to speak but suddenly stopped when she heard the garage door open.

"Stay there," she whispered, shoving David into the closet.

When her father entered the study, he looked at her in shock, mouth agape. The white hair on the top of his head was unruly, as if he had been running his fingers through it.

"Thank god you're safe!" he said. "You scared the hell out of me. How did you get back here?"

Her answer was as cold as ice. "Why don't you answer my question first?" she replied, reaching inside her backpack and pulling out her cell phone and her laptop. "Do these look familiar?"

Instead of answering, he stared at her blankly while she shook her head in disbelief.

"I can't believe you'd sacrifice my life so you could attend a stupid racist demonstration. What the hell were you thinking?"

"I had no idea that it would turn out the way it did," he answered. "All that matters to me right now is that you're safe."

She could understand nothing, think of nothing and feel nothing, except disrespect for him, disrespect that she had never felt until that moment.

A shadow of guilt darkened his eyes and he sank down in his chair.

"I don't know how many times or how many ways I can say I'm sorry."

"It's a little too late for that. All I want to know is how you got involved with that officer—ah—"

He started to answer but Officer Toomey limped into the room and interrupted their conversation.

"I'll answer that question," he replied, his voice gruff, his brows drawn together in a frown.

"He's a proud German, just like me. Perhaps he never told you that your great grandfather's last name was Crossman and that he owned a weapons factory in Obendorf, Germany, during World War Two."

His caustic words caused her heart to beat so fast she knew she'd pass out if she didn't calm down.

"Yeah, so what?" she answered angrily. "And who the hell invited you in here, anyway?"

He stiffened like an enlisted man saluting his commanding officer, his voice gaining an edge.

"Your father did, years ago. And it's the money that his late father left him that has supported Nazism throughout this country ever since the war ended."

She grabbed her father's arm and shook it. "Is what he's saying true, Dad? Tell me right now—is it true?"

He turned away and didn't answer. That gave Toomey enough time to spit out more racist rhetoric.

"There are many more of us who believe, as we do, that your father's generous donations will continue to help unite our organization and expand its membership. Then we'll get rid of everyone who doesn't conform to our way of thinking. Heil Hitler!"

Alesha gave him an angry stare and listened open-mouthed to what he said, scarcely able to believe her ears.

"If anybody ever finds out about this, my father will be impeached and I'll do everything in my power to see that you're fired."

He threw back his head and laughed without humor. "You've got as much chance of doing that as a monkey has of shitting in a toilet."

Her father jumped out of his chair. "OK, I've heard enough. Both of you; sit down and shut the hell up!"

David was peeking at them from behind the closet door. He stepped out, walked across the floor and stood beside Alesha.

Toomey recognized him while the judge raised his eyebrows in surprise. "How the hell did you get in here?"

"Alesha invited me. And it's a good thing she did because I recorded everything this lying bastard said."

"Give me that phone you fuckin' jailbird or I'll arrest you for breaking and entering," Toomey demanded.

Standing less than three feet away from David was a man who had caused him a great deal of trouble, a man who'd do anything to destroy him.

He handed Alesha his phone and gently pushed her behind his back, preparing for a confrontation.

Toomey reached out and tried to push David aside but he blocked it, and grabbed his arm.

Alesha screamed and her father yelled, "Stop it! There'll be no fighting in here!"

But being distracted while protecting someone you love can lead to serious consequences.

David promptly walked into a blazing sucker punch that rattled his skull. His knees buckled, but he remained standing so Toomey punched him again, this time on the shoulder.

The second blow sent him flying backward onto the judge's desk.

He rolled out of the way and brought his foot up just as Toomey advanced.

His eyes blinked, his nose exploded, blood erupted from his nose as David's foot landed on the side of his head with the force of a wrecking ball.

The blow turned Toomey into a semi-conscious 250 pound sack of flesh and bone.

He landed in a sitting position before his head jerked back and slammed into the floor.

David felt woozy but he managed to struggle to his feet and catch his breath.

Alesha yelled, "David, David, that's enough. You're going to get hurt!"

Toomey tried to raise himself into a sitting posture, but sank back on the floor. He reached behind his back, pulled out a 38 caliber revolver and aimed it at him.

"Back off, motherfucker," he said, "or I'll shoot you in every part of your body and then finish you off right between your eyes."

As soon as he stood up, Judge Cross threw himself upon his arm and dragged down the revolver which he had raised.

"What the hell are you doing?" asked Toomey. "I thought you hated blacks."

Judge Cross gave him an angry stare. "Hate never entered my mind. When you pulled out a weapon, you put my daughter's life in danger."

Suddenly, he was interrupted by a commotion in the hallway. He turned his head as four state troopers, two of them carrying assault weapons, rushed into the study.

The senior trooper moved with big, rapid strides toward Toomey a concerned look on his face. "Place your gun down on the desk," he ordered. "Then everyone—keep your hands where I can see them and don't move until I say so!"

After calm was restored, Toomey flashed his badge and pointed at David. "I'm a Natick police officer and I was trying to apprehend that—that—"

"Save it," the trooper said, cutting him off. "The FBI will be here in a couple of minutes. You can explain everything to them. Till then, all of you just sit down and relax."

FBI Agent Kay, along with two of his colleagues, soon arrived and began taking notes.

His gaze wandered over to David and Alesha.

"I assume you're David Furie, Chris Wellman's friend," he said. "And your girlfriend is Alesha?"

"Yes, sir," he answered, rubbing his aching jaw.

"It was a good idea for Chris to wait outside so he could dial 911. We've been monitoring calls made from this location for a couple of months."

He handed his cell phone to Agent Kay. "Before you and the State Police arrived, I was able to record a very important conversation. I think you'll find it very interesting."

"Thanks, I'll take it back to headquarters and give it a listen."

Judge Cross threw his arms around Alesha's neck, and without a word, he began to sob like a child. She hated to see him so dejected and sort of haunted looking.

"It's alright, Dad, don't worry. Everything's going to be alright," she said, resting his head on her shoulder.

A week later, the following articles appeared on the front page of every newspaper in Massachusetts:

Judge Hermann Cross and his wife of nearly 22 years, Amanda Sterling Cross, are divorcing.

"It is with great sadness that circumstances beyond her control have transpired which have resulted in Mrs. Cross's having to participate in a dissolution of marriage," her lawyer said in a statement.

***

Massachusetts' new POST (Peace Officer Standards and Training) Commission, a major part of police reform in the state, released the names of the first law enforcement officers it has suspended; among them was longtime Framingham resident Paul Toomey.

Toomey's suspension was prompted by accusations that he, along with four other officers, committed a felony.

"POST will suspend the certification of an officer who is arrested, charged or indicted of a felony and will revoke the certification of an officer who is convicted of a felony," said its executive officer Dan Salive.

The list of suspended officers will be updated periodically as these cases evolve and/or get resolved.

Chapter 49

Mr. Wellman was in a celebratory mood. He invited everyone to join him for dinner, during which time he praised David, Chris and Jenny for helping to alert law enforcement officials that a group of racists were planning to disrupt the May Day celebration.

"Let's start with Jenny," he said, toasting her with a bubbling glass of champagne. "Someone broke her car window to scare her off. When she reported the incident to the police and told them that she had also been attacked in front of Judge Cross's mansion, a red flag went up. That same evening, someone used Alesha's phone to butt dial David from the same location. Why do you think they did that?"

"Because hers was the only place they could find his number," Chris replied.

"Right—so it was either the judge or Toomey who made that call, because they wanted to make sure that she had no contact with him. They didn't want everybody to know about their plan, because then I guess it would have gotten out. And they didn't want it to get out."

"I'll bet it was the judge because Toomey looked like he had more brawn than brains," David said jokingly.

A ripple of smothered laughter circled the room.

"Then there's that amazing toss that Chris made all the way up to Alesha's balcony to find out if she was being held hostage," Mr. Wellman said.

Rose waved her hand to get his attention. "So, how did I fit into the picture?"

"Before he was immobilized, Mr. Parham was a smooth talker. However, when you cut through all the flowery words, he was nothing more than a first-class con man—a rascal. And like most con artists, he was adept at profiling people's psychological needs and desires."

"Despite his shortcomings, I'm willing to forgive him for that," she said.

"He doesn't realize it now, and I doubt if he ever will, but that business card that you gave to me was a big help."

"Oh," she said with a charming smile, "I thought it was the sexy way I sang *Bésame Mucho*."

Everyone laughed.

"That was also a big help. But that small piece of evidence made you an unwitting pawn in a continuing battle between law and order and crime and disorder. When you showed it to me, another red flag went up. That's when I thought it would be prudent to step back and set a strong boundary between what we were doing and the FBI's investigation into organized crime."

"That explains why you kept me locked up in your den and why that Wimpy guy tried to kidnap me."

"Exactly—except David stepped in and prevented that from happening. So let's all salute him for everything he's done to make life better, not just for us, but for everyone," Mr. Wellman said, proudly raising his champagne glass. "Oh, and by the way," he added, "now that all of the excitement has died down, what are you planning to do with yourself?"

David was a little embarrassed by all of the attention being given to him and his face flushed.

"Alesha and I are going to Miami to chill out for a week. When we get back, her father is going to need all the support he can get. I'll be right there by her side. In the fall, I plan to attend Harvard University."

His words were greeted with rapturous applause, and suddenly, he felt like his life was just beginning.

THE END

Other Books by Daniel W. Hood

Lobrigolin and the Forest of Fear (Book one, 2004)
Lobrigolin and the Book of the Ogham (Book two, 2008)
Lobrigolin and the Return of the Ghost (Book three, 2019)
Acre Beyond the Rye (2011)
Parasite (2011)
The Sophomores and me—A Love Story (2008)

Two innocent teenagers uncover a plot by several terrorist organizations to disrupt a patriotic celebration scheduled to take place in Boston, Mass.

With the help of close friends, they try to head off what could become a violent confrontation between the terrorists, the public, and law enforcement officials.